# WHO IS FRANCES RAIN?

Kids Can Press Ltd. acknowledges with appreciation
the assistance of the Canada Council and the Ontario Arts Council
in the production of this book.

**Canadian Cataloguing in Publication Data**

Buffie, Margaret
    Who is Frances Rain?

ISBN 0-919964-83-4

I. Title.

PS8553.U33W48 1987   jC813'.54   C87-094291-3
PZ7.B824Wh 1987

PRINTED AND BOUND IN CANADA BY WEBCOM LTD.

Edited by Charis Wahl
Typeset by Compeer Typographic Services Limited
Cover design by N.R. Jackson

Kids Can Press Ltd., Toronto

87 09 8 7 6 5

# Who Is Frances Rain?
## by Margaret Buffie

Kids Can Press Ltd., Toronto

To Jim and Christine —
For the past, the present and the future

# PROLOGUE

FUNNY, it's only been a few months since I met the people on Rain Island. School's started again, and sometimes those ordinary noises, like the rustle of books and papers, the shuffling of feet and the drone of voices, fade out and I drift back to Rain Island. Back to the little cabin under the pines.

Only when the bell rings to change classes do I collect my wits and slide back into the Real World. And just for a second or two, I wonder if I didn't imagine everything that happened this summer. All I have to do, though, is look at the flat gold ring on my middle finger and I know I'm not dreaming. Not then. And not now.

To be fair, I'd better warn you. If you don't believe in ghosts, and if you doubt that you could ever be convinced that they exist, it might be best to stop reading right about here. I wouldn't blame you. Before this summer, I'd have put down a story like this, muttering about flaky people who believe in some never-never land.

On the other hand, if you're a little more open-minded and want to stick with me for awhile, I'm pretty sure I can give you something to think about. Ghost-wise, at least.

# CHAPTER ONE

EVERY first of July since I can remember, my brother Evan, my sister Erica and I travel north by bus. We spend summer vacation with Gran at her cabin on Rain Lake, near Fish Narrows. It's north of Lake Winnipeg, where there's a huge wilderness of forest, muskeg and lakes with names like Chisel, Pakwa, Tramping and Weskuko.

Here and there around these lakes are small towns like Fish Narrows, towns that positively reek with the history of gold stakes, sourdough adventures and lonely traplines — and the ghosts that drift through those empty mines and forgotten trappers' cabins.

This year, we didn't go in the dusty old Northline bus with the rattling windows and squeaky seats. No, *this* year we had to go by car, and Mother's new husband Toothy Tim was behind the wheel. Not exactly where I'd have put him, believe me.

Mother and Toothy were going to be with us for most of the summer. I had no idea what had made them decide to come. Mother hadn't been to Rain

Lake in years. All I was sure of was that my yearly escape to the scrawny bosom of my old Gran had suddenly had a rusty wrench thrown into it.

The first few hours on the road, I had my nose stuck in a local history book. Gran had given me a few the summer before, about the past of the north, and I'd really liked them. After I'd got home, I'd actually found myself going to the city library and taking out as many as I could find on the area. Maybe someday I'll write a history book. My best grades have always been in history and English comp. I don't talk about my other subjects.

Lots of people travelled up north in the early nineteen hundreds, and even later, in the hopes of getting rich prospecting for gold and silver. Some scraped out a living, trapping during the winter or working for a local mine company, and prospecting during the summer months.

Most of them finally quit the north, fed up and broke, Gran said. Those that stayed, whether rich or poor, stayed because the northland had soaked into their blood and bones when they weren't looking. I think I'll end up being one of those.

Sometimes thinking about the past makes you forget things in the present that aren't so great. The present, I'd discovered lately, generally stunk. Reading the book made me forget newly married mothers and hairy stepfathers.

Toothy managed to hit his ten millionth pothole and I bounced back to the here and now, cramped in the middle seat of the station wagon. Beside me, in a sticky deep sleep, lay my little sister, Erica.

She'd just demolished two packages of chocolate rosebuds. The air smelled of chocolate, egg sandwiches and that hot car smell that always makes me sick to my stomach. Another six hours to go and I wasn't sure I'd make it. I sucked hard on a large Scotch mint and opened my window a little wider.

"Elizabeth! Shut that damn bloody window! It's like sitting in the eye of a bloody hurricane back here. Smells like a rotting fisherman's grave."

I threw a malignant look over my shoulder. Evan, my older brother, was stretched out along the back seat, one arm propped up on a tower of fishing boxes. He returned my look with his best sneer.

Sometimes, when I take a step-back look at Evan, I see him as others must: thin, small, almost frail looking, with thick sandy hair, a long narrow face and pointed nose.

Don't get me wrong. There's nothing feminine about Evan. No, Evan is the ultimate sexist teenage male. Ms Weaver, my English teacher last year, called a lot of boys that, and Evan definitely fits the bill. Front and back.

He was right about the smell, though. Our cocker, Bram, who at that moment was lying on my sneakered feet, was the source of the rotting grave. Somewhere on our trip, probably during our picnic near Grand Rapids, Bram had rolled in something pretty ripe. We'd washed most of it off, using Mother's shampoo, but the stink of putrefied fish guts, mingled with expensive perfume, had suddenly wafted up and around the hot car. I gave one hard pull on the mint before opening my mouth to give Evan a piece of my mind. Mother beat me to it.

"Evan. *How* many times must I tell you to *stop* using that inexcusable language?" She was using her long-suffering voice. "One *should* be able to show annoyance, and to *make* a request of your sister, *without* resorting to foul language."

"Yeah, Barf Breath," I muttered over my shoulder. Louder I said, "I have to have the window down, Mother. I feel sick. Why can't he take the dog for awhile?"

"Because he's your dog," Evan said. "And I'm not spending one moment with that mangy, flea-bitten, stinking, bad-tempered pound bait. See, Mother? Not an inexcusable word in the bunch." He chuckled, pleased with himself.

"You two have been *at* each other since *before* we left Winnipeg. We have just had a *heavenly* half hour of silence and I am *trying* to get some work done up here. I must have *peace* and *quiet*."

That's how my mother talks when she's ticked off. A kind of bored monotone, mainly through her nose. You can almost see the black pencil marks under some words. Her favourite request is always for *peace* and *quiet*.

Heaven only knows why she bothered to have one kid, let alone three. I'd always suspected that the reason all our names started with an "E" was because deep down she wanted to blend us into one kid. Preferably Evan.

The sickening thing about Evan is that he does everything right. He's an A student (he's skipped a few grades along the way and is already in university) and he even had his own concerto performed at the school of music this year. A hard act to follow.

Evan didn't like me and I didn't like him. We used to get along pretty well. We'd had to, with parents who spent half their lives in a courtroom and the other half at their offices. Maybe he stopped liking me when I shot past him in height. The poor guy's only five six to my five ten. It certainly wasn't because of my raving beauty. Who could be jealous of a stick-legged crane with a mop of mousy brown hair? No, it wasn't that. I think Evan stopped caring about anybody after Dad left for good.

# CHAPTER TWO

DAD had done his "now you see him, now you don't" trick about two years ago. He'd told us that we weren't to blame — that he needed time to be alone for awhile. That struck me as funny coming from someone who was hardly home anyway.

Mother didn't say much to us, except that everything was all right and not to worry. I thought she was pretty cool about the whole thing. Until the day he left.

I came home from school early because I had a sore throat. A pile of suitcases stood in the middle of the living room with Dad's coat folded neatly over the top. He was sitting on the edge of the couch, talking to Mother in a low voice and using lots of hand gestures. Mother was sitting straight-backed on the matching chair.

She just looked over his head as if he'd already gone, her ankles tight together and her thin hands gripping the side of the chair. It reminded me of something he'd said once during an argument. He hadn't been home for a couple of days again, and

I'd heard him say, "Why can't you loosen up a little and accept me for the way I am? Christ, Connie. You're so bloody starchy it's a wonder you don't stand up to sleep."

She'd looked at him and replied, "How do you know I don't? You're never around to check. How have you been sleeping lately, Carl?"

This time he was going for good. Neither of them noticed me standing in the hall. He loaded the luggage into the taxi waiting outside. The absolute silence in the house afterwards had been awful to hear.

Everything quietly fell apart after that, like a slow leak in a balloon. Mother had gone right on working throughout the days that followed, digging herself deep into court transcripts and hearing dates. I think I grew two inches and I *know* my grades went down the tubes. Evan stayed away from home more and more and his grades went up even farther. I guess little Erica got the worst of the deal — her first day in grade one without a mother or father to cheer her on, and a crotchety next-door neighbour as an after-school baby-sitter.

Now, it was Mother who came home late. After her supper, she'd close the door in the den and work. When Evan deigned to come home, all he ever did was practise his flute. I played Cinderella. It had been left to me to get dinner ready every night, to rescue Erica from the prune next door and to chase the dust bunnies up and down the hallways with the vacuum. I had been about to

13

demand equal rights with Mozart McGill, when something happened to change things.

Exactly three months before school holidays, Mother had got married. We hadn't even known she was going out with anyone. She seemed to spend all her time at the office or in her den — except for the one night a week when she took French lessons. That's where she met Toothy Tim Worlsky. Some big romance. Not even a Saturday night drive-in that we knew of.

To be fair, she didn't just up and marry the guy and bring him home like a box of doughnuts. But she came pretty close. She informed us one night by calling us into her study, lining us up in front of her like delinquent kids in a principal's office and then dropping the bomb. We'd stood like the Three Stooges with a collectively frozen pie in the face.

"I will not accept opposition from any of you," she'd said, looking intently at the desk top. "I will not ask you to love him. Or even like him, for that matter. I will, however, expect you to treat him like a guest in our home. If, after you know him better, you decide you like him, so much to the good. If you do not, keep it as quiet as possible. He will not pretend to be your father. You already have a father." She hesitated. We waited. She took a deep breath and swallowed. "I will continue to be the authority in this house as far as you three are concerned. However, if he asks you to take out the garbage, or mow the lawn, or something equally domestic, you will do as you are directed. Any conflict of interest will be brought to me. Tim and I are getting married in two weeks. He has invited all of us to dinner tomorrow night so that he can meet you. We will all be there.''

Just like that. Take it or leave it. And *every* word underlined. Evan had stared at her as if she'd suddenly turned into an electric can opener, then without a word, he'd turned and stalked out of the room. Erica snivelled. As usual. I stood holding her hand, staring at my mother, my brain set in neutral.

She and I'd never been particularly close. But I'd always admired her. From a distance, you might say. I used to imagine her changing my diapers, or feeding me strained carrots, or reading me Dr. Seuss, but it never really settled in full colour in my mind. Yet, she must have done all those things, at least till she'd gone back to work.

For a split second, I thought I saw something like an awful weariness and a plea for understanding, all mixed in with embarrassment, on that pale elegant face. I took a step towards her, but before I could say anything, a cold hard look slid over her eyes and she looked away. Taking Erica by the hand, I walked stiffly out of the room. She could stew in her own ice cubes.

So Mother and Tim Worlsky got married. The poor guy didn't stand a chance with Evan and me. We made it more than obvious that we had no intention of making his stay pleasant. We could only hope it would be short.

What a letdown. Instead of reacting to our carefully aimed pokes and sneers, he simply moved in

15

his records and books, hung his shirts and pants in Mother's closet and started right in baking after-school cookies and tuna casseroles — that stupid grin never once leaving his face.

Something about his size kept us from being outright vicious, but we worked hard at the little things, like ignoring his presence when he walked into a room, and grimacing at everything he cooked, as if it smelled of rotten eggs. Come to think of it, making his life miserable was the only thing Evan and I had agreed on in a long time.

The man was really a pain. By the time he moved in, we'd got used to eating dinner without an adult hanging around inspecting the vegetables we scraped into the garbage. Now we had *him* spooning horrible piles of green leafy stuff all over our plates.

Evan and I had also got used to eating in silence, threatening Erica with lima beans if she got too noisy. Now, we had this long-armed anthropoid picking his teeth and demanding to know how our day went. As if he really cared.

Evan usually circled him like a wary wolf anytime they met in the same room. For myself, I cannot tell you how much I hated the way he took over everything. When he started vacuuming up my dust balls without even asking me, I cleared out. I started hanging around my friend Doreen's house after school. She was a good student, and because I had a bit more time to spend on homework, my grades went up a little. It had absolutely nothing whatever to do with *him* being around.

Now, having King Kong around trying to be camp counsellor was bad enough, but to make matters worse, we found out he was a potter and would be working in the house every day. When he set up a studio in the basement — potting wheel, clay, plank table, kiln, the whole bit — I knew it was not going to be easy getting rid of him.

Don't get me wrong. I have nothing against artists. I like to draw and have a pile of grubby sketchbooks filled with stuff. Gran says that I could probably be an artist someday, if I stick to it. She wished she'd stuck to the sketching she did as a kid.

Sometimes, when Tim wasn't home, I'd go downstairs and feel the blocks of clay, smell the earthy smell of the workroom, look at his drying pots, and I'd get more and more angry — partly because I wanted to make pots, too, and knew I'd never ask him, and partly because I could see how good he was. He sold his stuff all around town. A regular Picasso of Pots.

I couldn't help wondering what Mother saw in him. And vice versa. She's always liked antiques, see-through china, water-colour paintings — stuff like that. She looks like that, too. Kind of fragile and a bit stuffy. Tim is big with a full red beard, sugar-cube teeth and a deep grumbling voice. Like nails on a chalkboard.

And the man was a wimp. Once I caught him secretly wiping his eyes watching some corny old movie on television. He'd even sniffle over those "call-home-long-distance" ads on the tube. My mother *never* sniffled.

She liked sole in white wine sauce; he made stew and dumplings. She liked lemon souffles; he was big on bread pudding. It must have been a crack on the head or some sort of perverted lust that threw *them* together. The mind boggled.

For awhile after they were married, Mother came home earlier. They'd take Erica to a movie or go out for dinner. Mother looked almost happy. She even laughed out loud a few times.

But then Dad called one night. I don't know what he wanted, but Tim and Mother had a shouting match in their room afterwards. I couldn't believe my ears. My mother had never yelled, not even when Dad told her he was leaving.

I wonder now if Dad asked to come back, because Tim hollered that she owed that bastard nothing, and what kind of a hold did he have on her anyway?

"The man walked out on you and three kids, for God's sake," he bellowed. "And hardly a word for two years. He's the one who's wrong. Not you. When are you going to figure this out?"

After that, Mother came home a little later every night. Tim seemed to take it all right, but a few times I caught him looking out the front window at night, shoulders slumped, hands in pockets, waiting for her.

It was his idea for all five of us to drive up to Rain Lake for the summer. Mother hadn't had a holiday in years, and although she'd put up a fight, he'd come out the winner. Temporarily, I was sure. They hadn't had a honeymoon yet and this was *not*

18

going to be it. The romance was definitely over. They hadn't said a word to each other, except "Pass the coffee," or "Stop at the next picnic site," since we'd left the city.

I should have been gloating, I guess, but instead I felt something that smelled like guilt at my part in the whole miserable business.

By now, you could be thinking that Tim seems like a nice guy and I'm a jerk. But at the time, I saw him as a big sliver under my nail. Someone who'd pushed his way in without asking. And how could we be sure he wouldn't clear out, too? Why waste time on someone when they could just as easily walk out? Like Dad did.

It's funny, too. Because inside, there's a me that's actually very nice, an almost grown-up, thoughtful me. Being with Gran made it easier to be that Lizzie. Evan and Mother and Tim seemed to bring out the me I wasn't too crazy about.

In the car that day, I only knew that I didn't want Mother and Tim around with their long faces and adult problems. They were going to ruin everything. I just knew it.

# CHAPTER THREE

WHAT with all the pit stops, doggy stops and nearly-out-of-gas stops, it was almost dark by the time we rolled through Fish Narrows. I'd fallen asleep somewhere near Minago River and I woke up groggily, feeling as if someone had crammed cotton wool into my head while I was asleep.

All five of us peered dismally out of the dusty car windows as Tim slowly wound his way along the narrow, private road that ended at Pickerel Bay Lodge, about fifteen miles from town.

"Aren't we going straight to Gran's?" asked Erica plaintively. Her hair was sticking up and her eyes were puffy with sleep. She pulled irritably at her new red shorts. Tim had bought them for her. And to go with it, fashion experts, a striped pink and orange shirt.

"Don't you ever listen, Chubber?" drawled Evan. "It's too late for Terry to be out on the lake at night. She's meeting us at the landing dock on Rain Lake tomorrow morning. Just like she does every year."

Erica glowered at him. "I forgot. And don't call her Terry. She's Gran. And don't call me Chubber, you weirdo!"

That's Evan all over. Mr. Personality. Erica still had what Tim called baby fat. He was always telling her that she'd outgrow it. But the way Erica ate, I doubted it. Gran was a great cook, so maybe it was just as well he'd bought the shorts three sizes too big.

"That's enough, Erica," said Mother wearily. "May Bird at the lodge will give us a decent meal and a good bed to sleep in. Maybe then your good humour will return."

You'll notice, of course, who got the blame. Not Evan. Never Evan, unless he used inexcusable language. Calling someone Chubber wasn't inexcusable, I suppose.

Erica looked at me and I winked. She winked back, with both eyes, and flopped back in her seat. A smudge of chocolate stretched from her mouth to her round chin. She looked like a sad little clown.

When the car came to a final lurching stop, I threw Bram and his fishy stench out the door. He ran around in crazy circles before lifting one expensively perfumed leg and spraying the nearest tree.

I stepped out of the car, adjusting my jeans and damp T-shirt. Pickerel Bay was shimmering ahead in the dusky light. A huge German shepherd loped around the corner of the lodge, making ominous rumblings deep in his throat. Bram's tail stood straight up, quivering. Tim edged back into the driver's seat and slowly closed the door. What a man.

"Hi, Silver," I called out, letting the snarling beast hear my voice. He danced up to me, a soft sloppy look on his big-bad-wolf face. While I patted his gargantuan head, Bram ran back and forth between his legs, finally nipping his throat in frustration. This got some attention and the two dogs raced off into the night. Tim nonchalantly inched his way back into the open. My hero.

We stretched and yawned — all except Mother. She never stretches or yawns, or looks crumpled or tired or sweaty. Tim looked as if a mugger had rolled him for his wallet.

The tall silhouette of a man appeared around the same corner that Silver had come from. As the shadow came closer I got the shock of my life. It wasn't a man at all. It was Alex Bird. His aunt and dad ran the lodge, and Alex spent his summers repairing motors, chopping wood and guiding fishermen to choice fishing spots. He's a year older than me, and he and Evan always fished together when Alex had the time.

When I was smaller, I used to beg to go along, but it was always no girls, no girls, no way. Sometimes Gran made them take me. That made them mad. Alex, a short fat kid for most of his life, figured it was his mission to tease me until I cried. Naturally, Evan helped out.

Last year, Alex had added on a few inches, but was still pretty hefty. Now, I figured he must have stretched up five inches and dropped twenty pounds. The only thing I recognized was his big hawkish nose. It seemed big noses weren't the only thing we had in common any more. This year we both towered over Evan.

Alex aimed his light at each of us in turn. For some reason, I thought he shone it a little longer on my face than on the others'. Normally I would have said hi, and then something rude, but my tongue had turned to wood.

"So, if it isn't the McGill family. I heard you were all driving up this year," he said. "Aunt May's had her eye pressed to the back window since dinner."

"It's Alex, isn't it?" asked Mother. "Well, Alex, I hope we aren't so late that we've caused any inconvenience for her or your father. My husband, Mr. Worlsky, is a very slow and cautious driver." She made it sound like a learning disability.

"No problem."

"In that case, could you give us a hand with our overnight bags? You too, Evan."

"Sure thing," said Alex, brushing past me.

"Evan?" said Mother.

Evan was walking towards the lodge, waving away mosquitoes with a paperback book. "The hired help can do that surely," he said. "Isn't that what we pay them for?"

My shrimp of a brother had taken one look at Alex and was eaten up with jealousy. Tim made it to his side in a half dozen long strides. In the dimness ahead, I heard the menacing murmur of Tim's voice and saw Evan pull away from the ham-hock hand on his shoulder. Could it be that Tim had finally threatened to push in my brother's snotty little nose?

"Aren't you going to say hi?" asked Alex, when Evan had slouched back to the car. "Or don't the upper classes speak to the help either?"

Evan reached into the trunk. "Hi," he muttered.

"How about you, Stringbean? Don't I get a hello from you either?" Alex looked straight at me with a wide grin.

The year before I would have peered down at him. Now, we were eye to eye. "I thought I did," I said.

He shrugged and ran a hand through his dark straight hair. "Maybe you did. All I can hear are these stupid mosquitoes. Don't just stand there, Stringbean. Hoist some bags. May's kept the dining room open for you guys."

I grabbed a couple of bags out of the trunk and followed him into a side door. A few minutes later we were settled around one of the large wooden tables. Evan had strutted towards us like a little crown prince, cocky as usual, but I had a feeling backed up by the flush on his cheeks that he wasn't sure how far he could push things this time and still get away with it.

I watched Tim watching him as he played the big man with the waitress, Alex's Aunt May and an old friend of Gran's. Even Mother's smooth forehead wrinkled when my darling sibling demanded ice in his water. He tipped back his chair. I willed it to fall over.

May looked down at the little twerp and a slow

smile creased her cheeks into fine furrows. "Sorry, kiddo, ice for cocktails only. Pretty limited space in our freezers. Besides, Evan, that's fresh spring water and it's plenty cold as it is. What'll you have, cookie?" she asked Erica, still smiling.

Erica settled on a hot beef sandwich, fries, apple pie and a vanilla shake. She always ate big when there were family tensions in the air.

After May walked back into the kitchen, Evan scowled. "Seems to me if someone asks for something, one should get it. Poor way to do business, if you ask me."

"Nobody asked you," said Tim in his low, easy voice, but something in his dark eyes made me uneasy. "And sit up properly." The last words cracked across the table.

The chair legs landed on the floor with a thud. Evan looked at Mother, who was looking at Tim, her eyes narrowed, her lips pursed. Then a slow, smug smile spread across Evan's face. If he kept quiet, Tim would come off as the heavy. Mother looked back and forth between the two of them before taking a long drink out of her water glass. Nothing more was said during the meal.

"Let's get some sleep," said Tim finally, breaking our long silence. There was a resigned tiredness in his voice, which kind of caught me by surprise. He always seemed to have the energy of ten men. Had we finally worn him down?

Our chairs scraped back from the table at the same time. Erica and I always shared a room. We loved this one overnight stay at Pickerel Lodge every year — it marked the beginning of summer — but that night I felt empty and exhausted. I trudged upstairs behind everyone feeling like I had a cord of wood in each leg. No one said good night.

# CHAPTER FOUR

THE next morning I wandered down to the kitchen where May was hard at work making the guests' breakfasts. I was able to grab a couple of baking powder biscuits dripping in honey before giving her a hand rolling biscuit dough. That way, I managed to avoid my sour-faced and silent family when they came down to eat.

May and I laughed and talked while we worked and for the first time in a while, I felt almost happy. I liked May. Her great-grandmother was a Cree who'd married a Scottish trader. May's father had been the principal of the local high school and a town councillor for almost thirty years before he died.

May and her brother Jack, Alex's father, took over the summertime business of the lodge after that. Jack was a history teacher in the same school during the winter, and he and his wife and Alex lived in a big log house down the shore. May lived alone at the lodge.

She's a little gnome-sized woman who always

wears moccasins on her feet and a sweet surprised look on her face most of the time, but she doesn't miss much.

I rolled out a ball of smooth white dough, watching to make sure I kept mine the same even thickness as hers.

"So you have a new stepfather, eh?" she said, in her deep musical voice. She put a pan of biscuits into the cookstove. "He seems a pleasant sort of chap. Like a big red bear. I sense a gentleness from him."

I rolled my eyes. "He's just a big, red pain in the you-know-where. I don't want to talk about him, okay?"

She smiled slowly. "Okay, Lizzie girl. But he might be just what the doctor ordered. Especially for Evan. Getting awfully big for his britches, isn't he?"

"You just noticed?"

She tapped one floury finger on her chin. "According to your gran, you've been housekeeper and mother in that family for the past year and a half. Maybe you'll have time for some fun, now. Maybe get better grades too, and go to college."

My hand holding the cutter stopped in mid-air. She laughed. "I'm only saying what Terry says. You know, you've changed this past winter. You suit your hair long and fluffy like that. Caramel brown we used to call it."

"Mousy brown, you mean."

"Why, you're almost pretty, you know that?" she continued, ignoring me. "Of course, your gran thinks you've got great possibilities." She smiled slyly.

"Gran talks too much." I caught her eye and grinned. "Well, she does."

"And if you'd stand up straight instead of slouching all the time, you'd look less like a skinny Hunchback of Notre Dame," said a voice from the back door.

Alex was lounging against the door jamb. An angry burning rush moved up my neck and flooded my face. One of my least attractive traits, I assure you.

"You must have won Mr. Congeniality at your school again this year," I said.

"Alex! You finished that load of wood yet?" his aunt asked curtly.

"Not quite. Hey, Stringbean, you think you might be able to beat me yet in a chopping contest?"

"Don't even imagine that you'll talk me into doing your work for you, Bird. I'm not that stupid any more."

He shrugged. "Too bad. You used to be a sucker for that one. You and Evan going fishing soon? I know a great place for big trout."

"You'll have to talk to his holiness. Besides, no girls, no way, remember? He might not even want you along. He's decided he's too good for the plebs of the world. Comes from riding his tricycle to university, I guess."

"Ah, he's always weird when he first gets here. He'll come around. And maybe, just maybe, we'll let you tag along."

29

"Don't do me any favours, please."

"Alex! Work!" May jerked her head towards the door.

He shrugged again, threw a grin around his big nose and walked away. May gave me a funny look, smiled to herself and took the biscuits out of the oven.

"You want one of these?" she asked. I shook my head.

Suddenly, a small figure scuttled across the room from the back door. "Well, by God, I know I do, and that's a four for sure, darlin'." It fell back in amazement when it saw me. "Well, I'll be...look who's here. Is it that time already? If it isn't the blessed granddaughter of my own dearest friend, Terry MacCallum, eh?"

"Hi, Harvey," I said, smiling at the bundle of grimy jackets and sweaters. A small grizzled head topped by an oily baseball cap stopped grinning toothlessly at me and eyed the crisp brown biscuits on the table.

He made a grab at one, but May was quicker. She reached across the table and hit him with the flat of her knife.

"And now what did you do that for? I wouldn't have taken more than one." The little prospector nursed his hand, his unshaven chin wobbling.

"I know you too well. You sit over there, like always," May ordered, pointing to a small table by the door, "and I'll get your breakfast."

He shuffled over to the table, where he took the position of a very good first grader at his school desk.

I eyed Harvey with a horrified fascination. There were even more long hairs growing out of the top of his nose and ears than there'd been last year, and his eyebrows grew like wild ground cover across the narrow forehead.

He pulled a pair of yellow false teeth out of one of his sweaters and slid them into his mouth. Giving them a couple of satisfied clacks, he started in on his plate of bacon and eggs. When he was through, he picked his teeth with a black thumbnail, took them out and dropped them back into the depths of his woolly pocket. A final gulp of coffee, a quick look around the room, and he was gone. May shook her head.

"That old buzzard owes me a pile of money," she said, her deep voice full of laughter. "Hard to believe he's got a bank balance that would choke a donkey."

We worked together for another half hour and May practically had to throw me out the door when Mother called that they were ready to leave.

Just before the car pulled away, Alex shoved a forgotten Adidas bag through the back window.

"I hear you're quite a fisherman, Alex," Tim said. "Maybe you'd drop around and give me a few tips."

Evan snorted.

"Sure thing, Mr. Worlsky. I'm usually over on Rain a few days a week. Maybe I'll see you there, eh, Evan?"

Evan shrugged. "Yeah. Gran'll want pickerel. Why not? See ya tomorrow, maybe."

"Okay. Tomorrow'll suit me. See ya."

Alex turned and walked away without saying a word about my going along. Nothing had changed. He was still a jerk, and I was still going to be on my own.

# CHAPTER FIVE

TIM bumped and rattled the car to the end of the dirt road where he parked under a clump of birch. The baggage had to be lugged a good two hundred yards along a footpath to a high rocky clearing along the shore of Rain Lake.

The sun glinted off an aluminum boat tied up at the dock. Gran stood up in the glare and waved. I recognized her straw hat and felt a rush of happiness. We all waved back and began to walk down the sloping rock.

Tim, hulking along behind me on the footpath, had managed to step on the backs of my sneakers about fifty times, so I was glad when we could spread out on the downhill walk. Evan ran down onto the dock and leaned over to swing Gran up and out of the boat. At least that was his intention, but it's hard to swing almost six feet of stringy muscle up and out of anywhere. They compromised. Gran hoisted one long thin leg and then the other over the edge of the boat, throwing an arm over his shoulders. Erica, who'd raced ahead too, caught her somewhere around the mid-section and the three of them, locked together, walked carefully onto shore. Evan's face was spread with the first real smile I'd seen on it in months, but when he saw the rest of us watching, he pulled himself together and scowled.

"Where's my Lizzie?" Gran demanded in her deep rusty voice, after receiving Mother's quick kiss on the cheek. "Get down here and collect your kiss."

I dropped my luggage and ran to her. Her strong arms pulled me close and I planted one on her velvety cheek.

"And this must be my new son-in-law," she said, over my shoulder. "Finally, we meet. What on earth made you decide to take this crew on for the summer?"

Tim was standing just above us on the sloping rock. In his new plaid shorts, his new flowered shirt, and his ugly white gob hat with a hole in the brim, he looked like King Kong goes to Hawaii. His ridiculous yellow work boots were turned toes out to the sides.

"And you must be my new mother-in-law," he said, lumbering towards her, hand outstretched.

"Call me Terry," she said, shaking his hand. "We may as well get a move on, Tim. We've got a lot of work to do around here, don't we?"

Tim looked over my head at Gran. I saw his eyes flicker, and then he smiled, a sideways twitch, as if he was sharing a secret joke with her. She chuckled and I hated Tim for pushing in between Gran and me.

"Come on, everyone, pick up some stuff and let's get a move on," Mother ordered, picking her way to the boat, carrying her straw purse and the dog's leash.

"Yeah, I'm not loading this boat by myself." Evan dumped a pile of fishing gear into the bow. He sat down on the edge of the dock, took off his sneakers and stuck his feet in the water.

"It wouldn't do you any harm, Evan, to take some of the heavier stuff and put it by the dock to be picked up later," Mother said. She was watching Tim and Gran suspiciously.

"So, how about Miss Lizzie over there?" asked Evan. "She's just standing around looking like she swallowed a live fly. Make *her* get going."

"Oh, shut up," I said, under my breath.

"She said shut up, Mama," said Erica helpfully.

"The usual symptoms of too-long-in-the-car-itis," commented Gran, picking up the cooler. "I've seen these kids get off the bus snarling like three little red foxes over a bit of cooked stew." She laughed, a thin squeaking sound, like someone opening a metal gate.

After we'd loaded the boat, I sat as far from everyone as I could on a little seat at the bow of the boat. I braided my hair into a long plait, holding it firmly over one shoulder.

The wind hit us with a wallop the second we nosed into the main body of the lake. The boat was a sixteen footer with a twenty-five on the back, and even though we'd left a lot of the gear on the shore, it would still take us awhile to go the three miles to the cabin. I turned around and faced into the wind, burrowing my feet under a pile of luggage in the nose.

We slid through the waves, slicing a thick wedge at the front and a deep trench at the back. The sun glinted off the choppy surface, searing my eyes with its dazzle.

Suddenly all my anger was gone. It was good to be back. Not just good — it was great. Let the others sit hunched against the wind. To heck with snotty brothers, pushy stepfathers and whiny sisters. I looked back at Gran.

She was holding on to her straw hat with one hand, the other gripping the motor's handle. Our eyes held for a brief moment and we smiled. Just like always, she knew what I was thinking. I was home.

# CHAPTER SIX

ABOUT a half mile from Gran's camp we passed a large island. There's also a smaller one between it and her place that we use for overnight camping and wiener roasts. The small one's called Little Island — not too original. The big one, Rain Island, was always off limits to us kids. There were too many sharp rocks below the surface of the water that canoes and small boats could smash up on.

I watched Rain Island pass by about three hundred feet away, high and rocky with a thick stand of pines at the centre. Their twisted tops reminded me of a fantasy castle's turrets. Maybe this year, it would be my castle, my retreat, where I could pull up my canoe and cut myself off from the rest of the world.

Light flickered in broken patterns deep in the secret places of Rain Island. Imagine. Whole hours away from Mother's closed face, from Evan's smart-ass mouth, and from a stepfather who hung around poking his nose into everything.

Now that everything's over, I keep trying to

37

remember if I felt anything unusual, a premonition or even a vaguely uneasy feeling when I made my decision to go to Rain Island. But no, I was just plain excited. It would be my secret place. No one would know I was there.

The sight of Gran's cabin brought me back to earth — well, water. When she nudged the boat expertly along the side of the sturdy dock, I hopped out and threw the heavy chain over the sawed-off tree stump on shore, where it landed with a clank and rattle. In single file, we carried luggage up the narrow path.

"Hey! This is great, Mrs. MacCallum," boomed Tim. "Why, it's the epitome of every wilderness cabin I've ever read about." He was gaping around and creating a traffic jam.

"I told you. Call me Terry," said Gran. "But it is beautiful, even if I do say so myself. My husband Bill and I built it, years ago."

It is a great place, large, low and rambling, with a shake roof, a stone fireplace and a thirty-foot, screened-in veranda — all in huge logs yellowed by layers of spar varnish and oil.

Tall pines and fat little spruce huddle close around it. When a wind picks up, they creak and rub against the walls and windows. That first day, though, the sun was shining and branches bobbed up and down, waving a childlike hello. The sun slanting through the pines along the path threw a pale greenish light over everything.

Evan beat me back to the boat and took off to get the rest of the supplies. I shook my fist at him. He

BLESSED KATERI CATHOLIC SCHOOL
LIBRARY

thumbed his nose back and gunned the motor up to full speed, riding the crests of the waves across the sparkling water.

I turned around to find Tim blocking the path again.

"Boy, this place is really something, eh?" he said. "I could live here forever."

"I wouldn't bet on it," I said out of the corner of my mouth. "City people start to get whiny after a day or two. Besides, Mother may have something to say about how long you stay. Here or anywhere else." That last bit was said under my breath, but loud enough.

When I pushed past him, I felt his eyes bore through the back of my neck. Wasn't he ever going to tell me to shut my fat mouth? How come I never felt satisfied any more after lipping off? In fact, I only seemed to get madder inside. Come to that, how come I ended up feeling like the creep? I kicked a stone angrily and hurt my toe. It seemed appropriate.

"Hey! Tim! Wait for me," cried Erica from the veranda. "I gotta do something. Gran's busy. I need you."

"Sure thing, Peanut," he called back. "Come on down!"

She giggled and hurried past me. "Coming!"

"Shit! If those two get any friendlier, I'll barf," I muttered as I slammed into the cabin.

"What's that you say, Lizzie? Are you using profanity in my house?" called Gran through the kitchen door.

I sighed and shoved my hands into my back pockets. Gran has a hearing problem — that is, until you mutter swear words under your breath. Then she has ears like the white-tailed deer that come to her backyard salt licks.

Walking slowly through the wide room with its bookcases, its overstuffed furniture and huge stone fireplace, I knew it was going to be hard to stay mad at anyone out here.

A trace of log fires, along with the cabiny odours of oakum, wicker furniture and warm sunny days, hung in the air. Yep. It was going to be hard. I'd have to work at it.

# CHAPTER SEVEN

"I SEE you've got a new set of outdoor steps," I said. "I like the crisscross pattern in the little logs under the handrail."

Gran looked up from her sandwich-making. "Alex Bird did it during the few decent weekends we had this spring. He's even better than his dad at building things."

I picked up a knife and began buttering bread. She pushed a bowl of egg salad towards me and said, "Well? How've you been?"

I shrugged. "Okay."

"Each of you looks like you lost your best friend. Except Evan. He looks like he'd like to kill *his* best friend. Okay, you say?"

"Yeah. Just okay."

I kept on working until the silence got to me. When I looked up, she was looking straight at me.

"Let's try again. How're things going? Have you heard from your dad?"

"A few notes. A couple of phone calls."

Gran pushed her face closer and narrowed her

eyes. "And no plane ticket for Evan? He was so sure that your dad would send for him."

"No."

"I figured that. But how are things generally around your place? Are you going to tell me?"

I put my knife down. "Okay, you asked for it. Things around our place generally stink. And it's been worse since *he* came. For awhile they got along and then one night they had this big argument, and Mother went back to being Ms Icicle of the Year." I looked around the kitchen. "It's good to be home. Boy, is it ever, Gran."

Her long, leathery face softened, and her eyes smoothed my hair, touched my face gently and looked deep inside me all at the same time. Everything poured out then. How Mother had started coming home later every night, how Evan was such a jerk, how Tim had moved in and taken over everything, and how even Erica had deserted me for him. But most of all, how I didn't belong there any more.

"Maybe I should get away, like Dad. To sort things out. Nobody would care if I was gone."

I sat down on one of the press-backed chairs that stood around the scarred old table and stared at my hands. I swallowed hard a few times to keep the tears back.

Gran leaned against the counter, not saying anything. I lifted my eyes just high enough to see the man's watch with the gold expansion bracelet she wore. It always hung loose on her skinny wrist and flopped all around when she worked. Sometimes, if her other hand's busy, I've seen her read the time practically standing on her head. It was Grandad's watch, given to him for forty years with the Fish Narrows Mining Company. I waited for her to say something. When I looked up, she just stood there smiling sadly down at me like a kindly crane.

A squeal from Erica and Tim's booming laugh came in the windows on the breeze.

Quietly, more as if she were speaking to herself, Gran said, "I like that fella. As soon as I laid eyes on him. I just hope your mother doesn't lose him."

"So what? Cripes, you've just met him. You don't know what he's like," I said. "But he'll be all over this place, getting in the way. I *know*."

"Do you really think you know?" she asked. "Or have you just decided you know the person you've made up in your mind? He's written me a few times, and I liked what I read. He's worried about your ma. That's why he insisted that she come here. She has to come to terms with your dad's leaving before she can start a new life. She thought she'd worked it through, but she hasn't."

All I really heard was the part about her and Toothy writing each other. They'd become friends without my knowing. He'd wheedled his way in with her before he arrived. The man was a slug.

"I'd like to start a whole new life," I said. "I wish I lived a hundred years ago." I leaned forward. "I wish I could live here with you."

"Maybe the best way to make wishes come halfway true is to work at the things you're wishing yourself away from. Wishes can become a prison."

I wanted to ask her to explain, but she was looking at something inside her own mind.

"Your ma and I are as different as day and night," she said. "She could hardly wait to get to the big city university. I grew up in city life and hated it. I came up here to teach, met your granddad and loved every minute since."

"After Mom and Dad got married, they hardly ever came up here to visit, did they?"

The look of sadness deepened. "Your dad's father was a big-time lawyer. So was your dad, as time went on. And now your ma, too. They were just too busy to get up here, I guess. And your ma always hated this place. Too isolated. You know."

"Funny, I can hardly wait for summer to come, so I can get here," I said.

She nodded. "I know, Lizzie girl." She began to cut the sandwiches. "Well, Tim walked right into a hornet's nest, didn't he?"

"I don't see why he had to walk in at all. Now, they're not talking to each other, and he'll probably take off. Just like Dad."

She put her hand on my shoulder. "I know how it is to feel left behind and left out. Being brought up by my grandparents was hard. They were too old to take on a young girl. Old-fashioned and strict. I felt all alone and angry. Sometimes it takes a while before you really know why people do things. Especially when they're your parents. Someday you and Evan will understand a little more."

"When Tim and Mother first got married, she

seemed different. You know...softer...a.
laughed more. Since their fight, everythin
mess."

"Give your ma a chance, Lizzie, give her time,
she said. "Give Tim a chance, too. You need him,
though you don't think so now."

There he was again, pushing in. "You're just like
Erica. He's not such a big deal. He never does anything except butt in. And smile and smile and
smile!"

She squeezed my shoulder. "Lord child, you can
be a pain in the backside. Take these sandwiches
into the main room and call the rest of the Happy
Gang for lunch." She rolled her eyes heavenward.
"Please let me get through this summer without
drowning one of them."

I threw her a haughty look and marched out of
the kitchen with my eggy tray. I thought I heard a
soft snort behind me.

# CHAPTER EIGHT

LUNCH was the usual dismal affair. Rain Island could only be better. I was lowering my little canoe, Water Beetle, over the side of the dock when Gran called out from the veranda.

"Lizzie! Don't go far, now. I feel electricity in the air. Could be a storm building up."

The lake was hazy under a trembling heat and the breeze had dropped a little. The waves were tiny ripples of black and silver. A fine film of wispy clouds was stretched low over the water.

Gran had a real feel for the weather most times, but it couldn't possibly rain on a day like this. Bram had plunked himself down on the floor of the canoe, and his flat ears with their fragrant curls shifted gently as we moved forward. Rain Island shimmered through the haze ahead.

When we neared its shadow, a breeze suddenly gusted around the corner and pushed at the Beetle. It was almost as if something was telling me to go back. I shifted my knees and settled down to keep us dead into the oncoming gusts. I hadn't come this far to give up now.

When we finally rounded the tip of the island, the wind suddenly died. I found a good place to land on the northwestern end, where a long rock sloped into the open waters behind me. A small break in the shoreline seemed made for the Beetle. I looked down. Could those strange dark shapes wavering below the surface be the broken pilings of an old dock? Maybe someone had actually lived on the island in days gone by. I liked that idea.

Bram hopped out and ran off, searching eagerly for new squirrels to terrorize. I pulled the Beetle up onto a mossy spot behind a clump of bushes and walked up the sun-scorched rocky slope towards the dark stand of trees.

The ground rose sharply towards the middle of the island. I came to the edge of the woods and walked through to the centre. Shafts of dusty yellow light cut through the ceiling of trees, laying patches of warm sunlight across the cool mossy bed below. The buzz of flies and piping of birds slowly faded, until I could hear nothing but my own breathing.

Bram was nowhere in sight. I opened my mouth to call him, but something made me stop. Everything was so peaceful. Ahead of me in a clearing, I noticed a flat rectangle of sunken moss, about twelve by sixteen feet. The rim around it was uneven and bulging, as if a green blanket had been thrown over a low open box.

It had to be the remains of a small cabin. I wasn't surprised. Somehow I knew it would be there. I crouched down at one corner of the box and pulled away a handful of moss. The pungent smell of moist red earth and rotting logs filled my nostrils.

Sitting down on a small flat rock, I cleared a spot where two logs had been notched to create a corner. I felt the uneven planes of the cut where an axe had chopped out chunks of hard white wood. Now, many years later, the logs were grey and spongy and crumbled in my fingers.

Who cut these logs? A trapper? A prospector? If I carefully dug my way around the cabin site over the next few weeks, it would be like an archaeological dig. Maybe I'd find some old bottles or tools.

Just then the sun disappeared. Everything was suddenly thrown into murky shadows. A cold mist seemed to push up from the ground around me.

I stood up and brushed off the back of my jeans. They were damp and soggy against my skin. When I leaned forward to put back the bits of moss, I heard a soft sigh beside my shoulder. My scalp prickled and goose bumps ran up and down my arms. Slowly and fearfully, I turned my head. There was nobody there. I started to breathe again.

All at once, a strong wind whistled a high-pitched warning above the trees, then swung lower to push around their branches. The trees slowly began to rock back and forth, their trunks swaying. I looked up uneasily, then fell forward when a rumble of thunder tailgating the wind brought something crashing through the bushes.

It was Bram. He ran as far as the edge of the cabin's buried skeleton. Then, hackles up, stiff-legged, he edged around the outside, looking at the sunken spot with rolling eyes. I had to laugh.

Bram hates thunder and usually turns into a bag of chicken bones at the first faint sounds of a storm. Overreaction is his middle name. He whimpered from a distance, his large brown eyes begging me to listen to reason and to get out of there.

"Bram," I said, "don't worry, boy. It's just a storm building up. Come here, boy, this way."

He was staring wild-eyed at something beside me, backing away and growling deep in his throat. When I took a step towards him, he bared his teeth and snarled.

"Bram? Cut it out!" Suddenly he was making me awfully nervous. "Stop it."

He growled again, showing the whites of his eyes, and began to mince around himself in a stiff-legged circle. I inched towards him, not daring to look over my shoulder where his eyes were glued.

A clap of thunder hammering above our heads did it. I scurried past Bram towards the rocky slope. He lunged after me, snapping and snarling like a rabid wolf.

We were both out of breath when we reached the canoe. Bram sat down beside it, a dumb bewildered look on his face. I pushed the Beetle into the water and held it steady for the killer dog. He walked around me first, sniffing and whining, put one paw on my leg and gazed adoringly into my eyes before climbing slowly into the canoe, shivering and shaking like an old, old man with a chill.

Across the bay the trees were shaking their branches over dark choppy waves, and the sky was full of black, swirling clouds. How could all of this have happened in the short time I'd been in the clearing? Was I going to sit out the storm or try for home? Sensible had never been *my* middle name, so naturally I pushed out from shore.

Crawling into the middle of the Beetle, I stayed on my knees and dug the paddle deep. By now, the wind was gusting in every direction, and because it hadn't made up its mind which way it wanted to blow, the waves in the sheltered strip between the two islands were still fairly small.

As I edged my way around Little Island's tip about twenty minutes later, a crack of lightning followed by a roller coaster of thunder threw Bram into another fit of the shakes. He crouched low on the bottom of the canoe, waiting for the Big Dog Catcher in the sky to come and get him. That was fine with me, because he'd been pacing back and forth, and the waves were getting bigger. I'd had to rap him a couple of times with the paddle and shout death threats to keep him from tipping us over.

The west wind had got a toe-hold between Gran's shore and us, and I knew that I'd never make it. The waves crashed against the rocks on Little Island. Despite my frantic paddling, we hardly moved, and my arms were aching so badly

I had to give them a rest. I raised the paddle, slammed it across the gunwales, and watched helplessly as Gran's shore steadily moved away from us.

# CHAPTER NINE

ANOTHER white-hot streak of lightning and deep roll of thunder collided right above our heads, and a musky smell of rain-washed pines and earth swept over us. Then the sky opened up. Huge drops of water splatted sideways into the white-capped waves. In a few seconds they became heavy curtains of pounding rain.

I tried paddling again — hard on the left and then the right, then hard left backpaddle, then right. Paddling hard going nowhere. I don't need to tell you that I hadn't brought a life jacket along. If Gran found out I'd be better off dead.

Dead?

This thought got the paddle going in double quick time. The wind was strong. I looked behind. The needle rocks of Little Island were waiting. I was doomed.

"Eeeelizabeth!" came a wavery voice through the grey wall in front of me. "Eeelizaaabeth! Can you seee meee? I'm over heere."

It took me a second or two to figure out that it

was a live human being in a boat, not some spook from Rain Island. The driver was sitting in a half crouch at the back of the boat, straining to see through the rain. It was Tim.

I was awfully glad to see him. Probably for the first time ever. Then it dawned on me that he hadn't seen *me*. The brim of his gob hat had fallen into his eyes.

"Turn the handle! Hey, Tim!" I screamed, standing up, and waving my arms. "Turn the boat! Push the handle. Turn the...turn the...."

As usual, he had to think this out. Of course, he had to push his hat back and wave. *Then* he turned the handle and cut the engine. That way, he hit us broadside instead of head on. If I'd been sitting down, I could have kept Bram and me from falling in. But I wasn't. So we did.

"Elizabeth!" I heard Tim bellow as I went under.

From where I was, heads up in the water, I could see he had hold of Bram's collar with one hand and the Beetle with the other. He hauled Bram in, flipped the Beetle over and dropped it bottom-up over the seats. I waved and swam through the slanting downpour and caught his outstretched hand. He patted all three of us in turn, just to make sure, I think, that we were actually in the boat.

The wind was tipping us up and over the waves towards Little Island. We'd have to move fast.

"Do you want me to drive?" I shouted, spluttering through the rain that was filling my mouth. "I know that motor. It's tricky."

"I'm okay," he shouted back. "I've been driving

it back and forth in front of Terry's for the past hour. I've got it down to a science." He grinned through his dripping beard.

"Put the handle just above start," I called, hopping to the middle seat to get closer. "Gran's fixed it so many times that it only starts in...."

"Start?" he asked, looking intently at the steaming engine. "Right. I wasn't putting it there before. It still started. Beginner's luck, I guess."

"Don't! Don't start it in start," I cried, then ducked as he stood up and gave the rope a gigantic pull, and another. And another.

Finally it dawned on him that all the muscle in the world was not going to start that damn engine. The rain didn't mind. It just kept pouring down like sand out of a dump truck. Tim, by this time, was looking helplessly around pulling and straining. I didn't want a sock in the side of the head, so I kicked him in the ankle. Hard.

"Ouch! Elizabeth, what the...."

"Get out of the way!" I shrieked in his face. "Unless you want to end up on those rocks."

Despite his size, he can move pretty lively. I set the handle and gave the rope a short sharp pull. The sweet sound of a bubbling propeller started below. Putting it into reverse, I slowly manoeuvred us away from the rocks. We turned into the wind like a bathtub full of water. Once I had the nose pointed directly into the force, I raised the horsepower and we sliced through the black, foam-capped waves towards home.

Tim was sitting hunched and forlorn on the bow

seat facing me, one huge arm steadying the little canoe, which was shuddering and heaving as it tried to fly. His hat sagged around his head, the rain sheeting off the brim into his beard. I couldn't believe the dumb jerk had headed out in this storm to rescue me. He'd never driven a boat before.

"Thanks," I shouted.

"Wha'?" he asked, lifting his head. I think I was as surprised as he was.

"I said, thanks. Thanks for coming. I was getting kinda scared out there."

He grinned and slammed the Beetle's bottom. And for some reason, his toothy grin didn't bother me at all.

# CHAPTER TEN

THE next morning I lay contentedly in bed listening to the thin chinking of a yellow warbler in the small birch beside my window. Then it dawned on me. What the heck was I feeling so contented about? I pushed my face farther into the soft pillow and sighed. If I got out of bed, I'd have to face my family.

I rolled over on my back. Dinner had been pretty bad again and to make matters worse, Alex Bird had been there taking the whole thing in.

He and Evan had spent the afternoon catching pickerel way off in the southwest corner of the lake when the storm hit. They'd found shelter with a young couple who'd set up a permanent home and planned to run a trapline in the winter. Lucky ducks. Imagine being able to live on Rain Lake year round.

They'd all played cards until the rain let up around six, and the two guys showed up just in time to polish off the chicken and potato salad and to get in on Act II of the Honeymooners Go to

Camp. Up to then, the rest of us had been making small talk. Very small. But at least Tim hadn't mentioned my fall in the drink, or that, when he'd rescued me, I didn't have a life jacket on. I think he didn't mention anything because Mother wasn't talking to him. Or to Gran. Or to me. She had just cut another slice of pie for Erica and was silently picking at her own when Evan decided the party needed livening up.

"So, when are you going home, Mother?" he asked, all innocence and light. "Did Alex give you the telegram? The one from your office? That's why he came over today instead of tomorrow."

Mother looked down at her plate and carefully cut her raisin pie into small squares. "Yes, he did, thank you. And I wasn't aware that I'd given you the right to read my mail."

He shrugged. "I just assumed it was important or they wouldn't have sent one. So, when are you going back?" He looked at Tim and back at her, like a cat teasing two mice.

"No one's going anywhere for awhile, Alex," said Tim. "And if and when your mother decides to go, we'll let you know." He looked at Mother. "You didn't mention a telegram."

Ever seen anyone talk through clenched teeth and smile at the same time? It looked like it hurt.

Mother examined her pie. "It wasn't important. I'll go over to the lodge tomorrow and give them a call."

Erica spoke up through a mouthful of raisins. "You *can't* go home, Mama. We just got here. Can

57

she, Tim? We're going to hike over to Cross Lake on the portage. Right, Tim?"

Mother looked at her fork. "I didn't say I was going anywhere." She placed the fork squarely in the middle of cut-up pie. "And if I go, it will be my decision. I have a job that demands my time. I can't just take time off whenever I feel like it. Not like some people." She stood up and started to stack dishes. "And some people don't seem to realize that I had a life before they moved in and I still have it. And what I decide to do, *I* decide to do. Not some people."

Tim stared at her through narrowed eyes. "I don't think anyone here wants to interfere with your career plans, counsellor. Just remember that your life includes a few more people than you, okay? Your decisions may...what is it you lawyers say...your decisions may impact on third parties."

"What does impact mean?" asked Erica.

"Impact? Oh, it means a collision of sorts," replied Tim, and when Erica frowned over that one, he said, "Or a bump. Like when you have a door slammed in your face." He looked at Mother.

"You mean like maybe a car crash?" Erica offered. "A real smash-up?"

"Yes, something like that," he said quietly.

Mother looked at him, startled. Then she turned and stalked into the kitchen. The sounds of slamming doors and clattering dishes echoed back to us. When Tim got up to clear the table, Gran removed some plates from his hands.

"I don't believe in women being the only ones in

the kitchen," she said quietly, "but tonight if I were you, I'd leave well enough alone." Louder she said, "Evan, you go in there and give your ma a hand. Erica can clear. Lizzie helped make dinner, so she and Alex can work on that new puzzle of mine in the corner. Tim, you and I need a drink. Whisky okay with you?"

Evan's stupid satisfied grin turned into a gargoyle-level scowl, but he did as he was told. He's never worked up the nerve to cross Gran.

When she walked across the room, I thought I saw a strange stiffness in her walk. She was rubbing her left arm as if it were hurting her. Could she be sick? I gave that idea a hard shove, but when she turned and I saw how pale her face was under the dark tan, a fine thread of worry pulled it back.

She mixed their drinks and sat down across from Tim. Surely, it was just the dull light that made her skin look so grey. Tim must have said something funny then, because she laughed and flapped her hand at him. He rumbled back. There was nothing to worry about, I told myself. Funny how we can snow ourselves sometimes.

"Hey! Earth to Lizzie. Earth to Lizzie. Come in please."

Alex's voice close to my ear brought me back to life. I looked into his dark eyes and blinked.

"Good," he said, "I thought you'd gone to another planet."

"Sorry, I was thinking."

"Do girls do that? I've oftened wondered," he said. "Don't strain too many cells up there, okay?

You'll need them to put together this puzzle. Your Gran picks the toughies.''

I pushed him aside. ''Did you know girls are better at puzzles than boys?''

''Oh, is that so? And how do you know that?''

''My English teacher this year hates men, so she told all the girls what to look out for and what we're better at. Puzzles are one of those things.''

I wanted to eat my words. Millions of tiny pieces were spread across the table.

''Well, this ought to separate the girls from the boys,'' he said, squinting at them. ''Sit down, and prove how good you are at *this*.''

I spent the next five minutes trying to make one bit of blue fit into a partially finished sky. Alex was working on a section of grass, and he was dropping pieces in one after the other. What I needed was a decoy. Erica's round cookie face came like a gift from heaven across the ocean of blue pieces. She sat down beside me and began fiddling with the little piles of sky I'd collected.

''Erica! I won't get any more pieces in if you keep mucking around in them.''

''Don't you mean, you won't even get one in?'' Alex said.

I snarled and pushed Erica and her chair to the other side of the table. Alex's hand dodged around, picking and fitting. The more pieces he fitted, the more I stared at the big hole in the sky. My brain had gone into neutral.

I never thought I'd be glad to see Evan walk into a room. The relief lasted about two seconds. He lounged up to us and bumped the table with his hip.

"Hey, Birdie, let's go to my room and play cards. Get away from the riffraff," he said, rolling his r's with disdain.

"Huh? Yeah. In a minute," Alex said, handing me a piece and pointing to a spot by my left hand. "Look, kid, I'll give you a break. Leave the sky. Do the apple orchard."

I took the piece of pink apple blossoms and tried to make it fit, but couldn't.

"Are you sure this goes here, or are you slowing me down?" I muttered savagely, trying to squeeze the rounded corner into a square space.

His hand closed over mine and moved it and the piece of candy pink to the right spot. "It fits. Maybe if you worked upside down, you'd see better. Like Erica. She's put in three. See?"

I didn't see anything but the slim brown hand over mine. It felt cool and dry. My own was hot and clammy. I pulled it away, found another piece and fit it in. Sheer dumb luck.

"There," he said, close to my ear, "with that in, we've started the hardest part. Your section has the most daisies. You girls do them. Real men don't do daisies."

"Then how come you're doing apple blossoms?" I asked.

"They're trees. That's different."

Alex took Erica's hand and showed her where to put the little bit in her hand. They grinned at each other. I'd never noticed how white his teeth were before.

Evan bumped the table again. A hard sharp push. Before we could stop it, half of the completed section fell to the floor, breaking into a crumpled pile.

"Evan!" screeched Erica.

"Hey, watch it, Bozo Brain," said Alex. "Your gran'll kill us."

Evan checked over his shoulder. Gran and Tim were busy talking. Feeling safe, he gave each of us our very own nasty sneer before saying, "Are you going to leave these wretches and retire to my room to play poker or what? Maybe you *like* playing finger-feelings with Elizabarf?"

I knew I was blushing. I hated it. "You are *such* a creep, Evan." He grinned.

"I can think of worse things to do," said Alex. "Like being pushed around by you." He leaned back in his chair. "Are you running for jackass of the year or what? Have you given any thought to becoming human again?"

"And what is that supposed to mean?" Evan's little beak of a nose looked suddenly pinched as if it had picked up a smell it didn't like. "Forget it, Birdie Boy. I've suddenly lost interest in cards. The company definitely bores me."

He stomped out, his skinny shoulders hunched forward in anger. I felt almost sorry for the poor schmuck.

It took us about half an hour to fix the puzzle, and a few minutes after that, I watched the light from Alex's flash bob down the trail towards the dock. We hadn't said much during the clean-up and had muttered good-bye at the veranda door, but now I saw the light hesitate, then it turned and shone on me.

"Say, how come you didn't come with us today?"

"I was out in the canoe. Besides, you guys never asked me."

"I asked you when you were in the kitchen with Aunt May."

"You call that an invitation?"

"Since when does anyone need an invite to go fishing?"

"No girls, no way, remember?" I reminded him.

"Oh. Right. Next time I'll send an engraved invite."

"How nice."

"Or I can ask you right now. You can come next time. If you want."

"And next time, I may be terribly busy. Check with my secretary and we'll get back to you." I marched into the veranda.

He laughed and shouted, "Will do, Ms. McGill. My secretary will contact your secretary and we'll do lunch."

I listened to the fading drone of his motor for a few minutes wondering what I really thought of this new Alexander Bird. The word interesting definitely came to mind.

# CHAPTER ELEVEN

"BUT that was last night," I said aloud, pushing my bare feet into the cool corners of the covers. "And today is today, and I've got work to do on Rain Island."

I forced myself to concentrate on the gear I'd need to excavate the cabin site. In the pile of history books I'd read over the winter, there had been a pamphlet put out by the city museum showing how a group of their archaeologists had dug up the remains of an ancient Indian village. Maybe I could be an archaeologist some day — if not a trapper or a writer or an artist, that is.

I'd need a trowel, a shovel, a tape measure, some strong string, my sketchbook, a cardboard box or two, an old screen and my lunch. For starters.

A few minutes later, after washing up in last night's basin of soapy water and dressing in jeans and T-shirt, I walked down the hall towards the kitchen. Raised voices floated towards me along with the smell of frying bacon. Mother and Gran were arguing. I peeked around the corner.

"...so don't go lecturing me on being a better wife and parent, Ma. You should be in Toronto lecturing Carl on good parenting. He's the one who left town."

Her shoulders were up near her ears and her thin hands were clenched in front of her. I sincerely hoped that she didn't do that in court when she was arguing a case. No one wants to be defended by Squirrel Nutkin.

Gran was calmly pouring herself a cup of coffee, but the hand holding the cup shook a little and her voice had gone down two octaves. It always does when she's mad.

"I'm not lecturing you, Connie," she said patiently, "but you might have gone blueberry picking with Tim and Erica. That's all. They really wanted you to go. He's very good to her. Spending time. You're practically handing her over to him to raise. She needs you. So does he. He's good to you, too."

"I am *so* sick of hearing how good he is," Mother said, fiercely. "What the hell am I? Chopped liver? I should never have married him. Tim pressured me too soon and now he expects everything to be just rosy. Don't you see? I wasn't ready — it's more than I can give. And now Carl's calling all the time. Wanting to talk."

"Talk's cheap, Connie. Tim is here."

"Thank you, Ma, I didn't notice."

I had moved into the room, drawn by a dreadful curiosity, but began to edge out again, trying to be invisible. Funny how the minute you try to disappear, everyone sees you.

"Elizabeth! Stay right there," Mother demanded. "Tell your Gran. Go ahead. Tell her about Tim. You and your brother have made it very clear how you feel about my new husband."

"Uh...he's okay," I said. "He just takes getting used to. He did come out in the storm to get me. And he'd never driven a boat before. He could've...."

She stared at me, her eyes bulging. "So now he's Mr. Wonderful, is he? That's just fine. After three months of treating him as if he's a social disease."

"Don't worry." I tried for a joke. "Evan'll still treat him like that. Tim won't get spoiled."

"Very cute. Now Tim is just fine! And I suppose I'm not." She turned to Gran. "Don't give me that look, Ma. I come home every night. I work hard. I like my job. Why can't I do it, without being suffocated?" She shook her hands in the air as if they were wet. "Or feeling guilty."

Gran cut in. "I think that's enough, Connie. Maybe what you need —"

Mother brought the flat of her hand down on the counter. "What I need is to be left alone! What I need is *peace* and *quiet!* What I need...."

"Listen to yourself. What you need...what *you* need. What you need, Constance, is a kick in the backside."

Mother sagged against the counter. "You just don't understand, Ma."

Gran's voice softened. "I think I do, Connie. Carl left you. You've hardly seen him for two years. Now, for some reason, he wants back in your life. You have a choice to make. But, Connie, he's the loser. Not you. It wasn't your fault. But you're starting to lose everything, too. By closing yourself off. Shutting out Tim. You have to decide. Tim won't leave you. Not like Carl."

"How do you know that? You never understood, Ma."

Her eyes looked so stricken and bewildered that I wanted to put my arm around her, to protect her. I looked away. When I looked back, she was gone. The back door slammed.

Running to it, I saw the tail of her red sweater disappear into the foliage along the path leading to a rocky ridge behind the cabin.

"Best to leave her," Gran said, behind me.

"I've never seen her like this," I said. "Not ever."

"She needed to let go a little," Gran said. "She's been holding it in too long. Your dad never learned to share. Neither of them learned to give. Everything's always come easy to Connie. Let's see if she's ready to give some of it back."

# CHAPTER TWELVE

WHEN I left the dock to paddle over to Rain Island, Mother still hadn't returned, and Gran refused to say anything more. Maybe I should have been more upset, but I was actually relieved. Relieved, I guess, that my mother could yell and carry on like real people. I preferred that to white-faced, silent anger.

I wondered what decision she'd make about Tim. And Dad. He'd never been around much, so I couldn't pretend I'd missed him. But Tim was different. Hard to believe that I'd actually miss someone I thought I'd hated for three months. Maybe I was a born-again stepdaughter.

Lucky for me Gran hadn't even asked where I was going. I'd left her taking out her frustrations chopping wood behind the cabin, waiting for Mother.

The sun was high and the dappling shadows of the trees had moved across the landing rock by the time I'd carried the gear bit by bit to the site. The waves on the lake were pale silver and glittery in the distance, and birds sang high in the trees. Mother's problems drifted away on the morning breeze that cooled my face. Suddenly I felt ready for adventure.

Walking around the site, I chose a spot that faced the lake through a wide break in the trees. It looked as if that view had been around a long time. Maybe the builder of the little cabin had even put a window overlooking this stretch of open water — as good a place as any to start. It was all going to be hit and miss anyway.

I hammered four tent pegs into the ground marking off a square four feet by four feet, running a string around the pegs the way I'd seen the archaeologists do in the museum pamphlet. Now I had a spot I could attack. If nothing happened here, I'd move on.

First I pulled up clumps of damp green moss and tossed them over my shoulder. Smaller plants, like blueberries and bunchberries, had all worked their way down through the sphagnum. The axe and shovel got a good working out on the snaky brown roots.

Only smaller plants were growing in the sunken space — not one tree had taken hold in the low green bowl. The tallest plants were a few clumps of fern near the back of the cabin. I decided not to look a gift horse in the mouth. I couldn't have hacked my way through anything bigger. Paul Bunyan, I'm not.

Bit by bit I pulled up clumps of dirt and roots, shaking them through an old screen window I'd brought with me. I wasn't expecting much at this point, so I was surprised when my trowel hit something that sounded kind of hollow. I poked through the dirt again and — thunk — the same hollow sound echoed back.

A whole layer of matted roots and soil, thick with the smell of rotting plants, lifted easily in one piece. I rolled it back. Underneath was the roof. The decaying bits of black and green roll roofing had once been attached to the boards below.

An hour later, I'd pulled out the crumbling boards and log stringers. Under the roof, I found pieces of broken glass and a rotting wooden casement. So, there *had* been a window at this spot. After I'd dropped the razor-sharp pieces into one of the smaller boxes I'd brought, I sat back on my heels and looked at my first real find. A small table-top. Not much, you say. But it was covered with tiny yellow tulips and blue polka dots. Now I ask you, what tough prospector covers his table with oilcloth painted in a tulip design? It had been nailed on with a neat row of copper nails all around the edge.

I carefully lifted it to one side. I was tempted to rip through everything, but the pamphlet warned against that, so I cautiously moved away more dirt and found a carved wooden table leg for my trouble. Dull blue paint chips peeled back under my thumbnail. I tried to imagine what it must have been like, sitting at the little blue table with its cheerful oilcloth covering, looking out over the lake and watching the seasons go by.

A large black beetle scuttled out from under another table leg wedged into the soil. Waving his long antennae anxiously in the air, he tried to pick up any murderous vibrations before disappearing under a clump of peat. I watched his back legs toss up some dirt and at the same time noticed a glint of something under him. I flicked him away and he disappeared into the moss. From the soft earth, I pulled out a large cream-coloured mug. It left a perfect imprint of itself in the dirt. I brushed off the lettering on the front: "Sparton's Root Beer, The Cream of the Crop, Est. 1889."

I crowed out loud. It wasn't even chipped. The inside was filled with muddy-looking gunk. I tipped it over, tapping the bottom gently with the palm of my hand. A small leather parcel fell to the ground along with some crumpled oilcloth and black dirt. I delicately opened the rolled piece of leather. It was stiff under my fingers, but still fairly flexible. The oilcloth must have protected it for all the years it lay underground.

When I was through, I held bits of oilcloth, a blackened piece of animal skin, and a pair of wire-rimmed spectacles whose small round lenses were dirty but unbroken. They looked smaller than those that a man would wear. They looked like kid's glasses. I put them on and looked around. The murky glass gave the scene a dull, gloomy look, almost as if it were dusk instead of a sunshiny noon.

Grinning idiotically, I tucked them into the pocket of my shirt. Before I could stand up, though, everything around me dipped and swayed. For a second, I thought I was going to faint. I put my head between my knees. The dizziness drained away almost as quickly as it had begun.

"Must be hungry," I muttered, shaking my head. "Well, kiddo, you deserve a break today, so get up and get away. For some lunch. More digging later."

I ate my picnic with my back against the trunk of a big jack pine overlooking the bay. The lake was sparkling in the noon sunshine and the warm breeze cooled my sweaty shirt.

"Next time, I'll bring my bathing suit," I said to myself, happily working my way through a tuna and pickle sandwich, two apple tarts and half a thermos of raspberry Kool-Aid.

When I leaned over to screw the lid onto the thermos, I felt the glasses shift in my shirt pocket and pulled them out for another look.

I buffed them on the tail of my shirt and put them on. At first, because they were someone else's glasses, I figured they were blurring my vision. But the thing was, my eyesight wasn't blurred — something else had happened. The summer sunlight and clear blue sky were gone. It was dull and misty, with low hanging clouds barely skimming the tops of the trees. And the distant shoreline had somehow changed to the hazy khaki and yellow of late autumn. Many of the trees were bare. Here and there a flash of red shone through.

When I pulled off the spectacles, another sudden

wave of dizziness ran through my head like an electric jolt. I had to sit down.

"I must be dozing off like Alice," I thought, shaking my head. "I'll be seeing the White Rabbit next."

As soon as my head cleared, I scrambled to my feet and picked my way cautiously back to the site. I stood a little way off, peering suspiciously around. It looked so peaceful.

I slid the specs out of my pocket, opened their thin arms and stared at them. The sensible Elizabeth side of me was telling the reckless Lizzy side of me that I was simply imagining things — a mood, a feeling that wasn't really there. But the reckless side, as usual, wasn't listening. She never does.

I put them on.

# CHAPTER THIRTEEN

NOTHING happened. I looked all around. Then, I happened to glance down. Far, far in the distance, I could see my sneakers. I wiggled my toes and the tips of the sneakers moved. The path, just to my left, was well worn and hardened, as if it hadn't rained the day before.

Path? There was no path on the island. Yet I stepped over onto it and my feet, distances away, lifted themselves and carried me along. I thought I could see the vague outline of blueberry bushes beneath the flat greyness of the path. Behind me, it stretched to the sloping shore. I turned and faced the cabin.

It was lower and wider than I'd imagined. I had just finished digging up a place of rotting mildewed logs. The logs in front of me were pale grey and silvery smooth, the roof over them covered in the green roll roofing that I'd found in bits and pieces a foot under the soil.

As I stumbled towards it, the scene shimmered, like a home movie on a hanging bedsheet screen.

The cabin was there and yet it wasn't. The background of my own world wasn't really there and yet it was. If you'd asked me later how I'd felt at that moment, I'd have told you how surprised I was I didn't drop dead from shock. But, in fact, I only remember shutting my open mouth and taking a few hard gulps. The glasses stayed on though. My bump of curiosity has always been much larger than my bump of self-preservation.

I mean, I knew that what I was seeing wasn't real, but I was also sure that I was seeing the cabin as it had once been. The path drew me forward and I walked along it, my feet now and again getting tangled up in the small plants behind its shadow. Once I tripped on a log that wasn't there. Or was it?

What I'd do when I reached the cabin that was wavering in front of me, I didn't know. As I walked closer, everything seemed to become clearer, more solid and more attractive, as if it was a magnet and I was a bit of metal.

The door of the cabin was made of rough boards, the door handle a simple carved block of wood with a metal latch. I could make out the coarse grain of the boards and the rust spots that had dripped down from the nails. But the weird thing was, I could also still see the outline of the trees that ringed the clearing behind.

A pain that had started at the back of my head when I'd first put on the glasses suddenly grew stronger. I shook it away before reaching towards the latch. When the pain came again, harder this time, I moved back a few steps from the cabin.

Pressure seemed to be building up inside my brain. I could feel it pushing against the backs of my eyes.

Shaking my head to relieve the pain, I saw something out of the corner of my eye — something that flitted around the dim light at the edge of the building. My heart beat in thick, sickening throbs. Someone was there. I listened and looked, my head crushed with pain. Again, I saw the flicker of movement, but now it seemed to be drifting behind me, out of my line of sight. The horrible thing was, I couldn't turn to see if it was coming closer. It was as if I was being held in a vise.

I tried to tear the glasses from my face but couldn't move my arms. The awful silence I had felt the day before once again hung around me, as if someone had dropped a deadening headset over my ears. Suddenly, I felt a terrible weight fall against my shoulders, a weight so strong my knees started to buckle under it. I fought to stay on my feet.

A whistling sound, like a giant's breath, rushed in and out through my head. My hand moved from my side, as if someone had taken control of it, and it hung in the air ready to take hold of the door handle. I watched in horror as its long paleness dissolved to a filmy mist, and in its place, a larger hand, brown and sinewy, reached towards the handle. A flat gold signet ring glinted in a far-off light.

I didn't wear a ring...I didn't wear...slowly, slowly, the pressure pushed me towards the door. The hand with the ring took hold of the handle and pushed the door open. Yet it was the other pale spirit hand — my own hand — that drew away. The muscles in my arm, driven by my terror, lifted it towards my face.

With every ounce of willpower left, I forced my eyes shut. It took all my concentration, for other eyes were also looking at the door, wanting to get inside the cabin. I knew I'd be pulled in, too.

When the scene before me was finally blacked out, it was easier to move my arm. I fumbled with numbed fingers for the glasses, and somehow managed to hook my thumb under the wire arm, yanking them up and off in one hard pull.

The glasses and I hit the ground at the same time. I lay for a long time with my back deep in the damp thick moss, waiting for the tall pines above me to stop turning, waiting for the dizziness and nausea to leave. I felt as if I'd been on the biggest ride in the fairground. Only it hadn't been any joy ride.

The top of my head felt as if someone had hit it with a hammer. Carefully I touched it. No bump. Just a tender spot. I winced and dropped my hand. It fell like a dead weight.

I'm not sure how long I lay there, gulping and gasping like a jackfish out of water, but when I did manage to stagger to my feet — probably looking like a drunk orangutan — I knew I had to get off the island. Archaeology wasn't any fun any more.

Not daring to look behind me, I stumbled towards the safety of the Beetle, stopping only long enough to pick up Gran's tape measure, the trowel and the shovel.

After I'd paddled away from the landing rock, I made myself look back at the island. The sun had that deep yellow glow of northern afternoon and its heat was lying heavy and thick over the water. The pines stood silent and still, keeping their secrets to themselves.

The smooth wooden paddle gripped tightly in my hands and all the familiar sights around me — the flashes of light off the waves, the rich green of Gran's distant shore, and a sharp-winged tern riding high in the shimmering heat — they all seemed to only heighten the feeling that maybe I wasn't really here any more, that somehow I'd become part of someone else's dream.

I shook my head. No. I had to be real. I'd read somewhere that if you pinched yourself hard and it hurt, then you weren't dreaming.

"Ouch!" I cried.

I was real all right. "So, if that's true, and if I'm real," I snuffled to myself, as I paddled hard for home, "then who the heck did I bump into on Rain Island?"

# CHAPTER FOURTEEN

IT'S amazing how a night's sleep, daylight and bacon and eggs can change a person's ideas on ghostly cabins and phantom hands. By the time I'd crunched my way through a fourth piece of bacon, I'd convinced myself that I'd fallen asleep on the island and dreamed everything. Like Alice.

I'd also decided that I would hang around home even if it meant putting up with Mother and Tim and Evan. Gran and I were sitting at the table, mopping up the last bit of egg yolk and slapping marmalade on our toast crusts, when two of the three walked in. The Happy Twosome.

Mother, in her silk housecoat and satin mules, muttered, "Good morning" and went straight to the coffee pot. Tim, vertical, but otherwise still asleep, slumped into a chair and mumbled on a cold piece of toast.

I'd already lost track of the number of heated conversations these two had waded through in the past few days. "Conversations" is their word, not mine. They'd fought for hours the night before. It seemed that Mother was *going home*, but according to Tim no one was going anywhere until certain things were straightened out. It was all very tense and getting worse when I decided to go to bed. I'd been hoping to see Alex that evening, but had finally given up in disgust. The whole day had been too much to handle.

Evan had stayed up trying to referee the "conversation" — or coach it — depending on whose side you were on. He was on Mother's, of course.

You know what was really strange? I actually found myself rooting for Toothy. Funny how his bungling up the rescue operation that day in the storm had given me a kind of protective feeling for the big dope. And I figured if he won, then maybe, like Gran said, Mother would win, too.

Now, watching them with a wary eye, I couldn't help wondering if they'd come to some sort of a decision. I was about to make myself another toast with marmalade, when Gran gave me a raised eyebrow message to clear out.

I walked slowly from the room keeping an ear cocked in case the row started again. I wanted to know who'd win round two. I was about to creep back and listen at the kitchen door, when I heard a loud scream down by the shore.

"Eaah! Bram! Let go! Leggo!" shrieked Erica.

I ran outside and found her, still wearing her pyjamas, chasing Bram in and out of the shoreline bushes, howling something about a daisy. She kept tripping over the legs of her oversized pyjamas into the sandy dirt. Tears ran in dirty trails down her cheeks.

"What's up?" I called. "Stop it, Erica! Bram! Hey, what's happening?" I caught hold of her.

"Bram ate Daisy! She's been eaten up!" Tears gushed.

I let her go and chased the dog down, cornering him inside Gran's woodshed. He lay on his belly, tail wagging madly, tongue slopping over his killer teeth.

"Okay, kid. You are in big trouble," I growled. "Out with it. Did you kill Daisy? Come on, cough him up. Grrr."

"Cough what up?"

I was down on my knees growling at a fat cocker spaniel, so it seemed only right to look up and see Alex frowning down at me. I grinned sheepishly, then scowled when I saw his wicked grin. Erica ran around the corner and threw herself on me, sobbing hysterically. We collapsed in the dust.

"Bram ate Daisy!" she cried. "Oooh! Poor Daisy."

"Who or what is a daisy?" asked Alex, mystified.

"Pet chipmunk," I said, struggling to my feet. "He gets sunflower seeds from Erica every morning. Or Gran. He and Bram have this game they play every year. You know, Bram threatens and Daisy teases. This time I think Bram called the game."

"Daisy's not a he! She's a she...and she's been murdered! I hate you, Bram!" She came closer. "Look in his mouth. Can you see her?"

We all stared at the golden sausage with the sweet face.

"Erica," I said patiently, "if Bram ate her, then she is not going to be in his mouth." I shook my head sadly. "Besides, she could have got away."

"But I saw her tail hanging out of his mouth!" she wailed. "Like this." And she wiggled her fingers in front of her lips. "Look in his mouth. She could be there. Look, Lizzie, please?" She was jiggling up and down, her voice pleading.

"Bram, com'ere," I said.

He looked at me, considering, then slowly dragged his belly over to where all three of us were down on our knees waiting. I examined his soft lips and yellow teeth. Not a sign of gore, not even a bit of fur stuck to a canine tooth.

Alex looked at Erica and smiled. "I don't think he ate Daisy at all. I bet he dropped her off on his run around the yard. I was watching and there was no way he had time to get in a good chew. He was probably so surprised to find her inside his mouth, I'll bet he dropped her right away. My dog does it all the time."

"He does?" she asked, wiping the dirt around her face. "You mean Daisy could have run home by now?"

"Yup. That's what I think happened," he said. "As far as I'm concerned, she's home right now with an ice pack between her ears, telling all her neighbours about her big adventure. Hey! You wanna go fishing, Erica? You too, Stringbean. I know a great fishing spot not too far from here."

Erica beamed wetly up at him. "I'll bet she *is* home. I'll go get my stuff." She waddled off.

"And wash your face," I called out. I looked at Alex suspiciously. "You mean to tell me that your big brute of a dog catches chipmunks and then spits them out safe and sound?"

"Well...he spits them out. By the time they hit the ground, they're usually dead as furry door-nails."

"Poor old Daisy," I sighed. Bram wagged his tail and gazed happily at no one in particular.

# CHAPTER FIFTEEN

A LITTLE while later, we were bobbing around on the water, our lines deep, and the motor putting slowly along. When we passed Rain Island, I looked hard at the stand of trees in its centre. Sitting there in the boat, chewing on an Eatmore and drinking a cola, I had trouble believing that anything strange had happened the day before. The Alice in Wonderland theory still held up. I'd almost told Gran about it after supper, but all that arguing kept me quiet. Now, I was just as glad. It all seemed so ridiculous.

We got back two hours later, with five good-sized pickerel and a couple of small perch. When she asked for lunch, I knew Erica had forgotten about Daisy. Alex followed us into the veranda looking hungry, too.

"Want a sandwich?" I asked him.

"Wouldn't say no to one. Wouldn't say no to two, either."

Evan, who'd been asleep when we left, was sitting on the veranda reading a book. He pointedly ignored us. Alex batted his feet out of the way and sat down on the end of the lounge.

"You guys want a lemonade or anything?" I asked.

"Sounds great," said Alex. Evan scowled at his book.

I shrugged and went to check out the food situation. Mother was still in the kitchen. A pile of dirty coffee cups, filled ashtrays, books and briefcases were spread all around the table. Gran was peeling potatoes and casting savage looks at her daughter's bowed head.

Tim was in the main room, slumped on a couch, reading a mystery book with a ferocious frown on his face. I felt like screaming a few dirty words into the air, just to see what would happen.

Over lunch, things got tougher. Gran and I gave up trying to talk to the store window dummies that looked like Mother, Tim and Evan. It helped having Alex there, though. He talked to Gran about plans for a new dock in the landing bay and to Erica about fishing, and ate his way through piles of roast beef sandwiches. Tim, who'd perked up a bit when fishing was mentioned, asked us how many we'd caught.

"Five," said Alex. "You guys can have those. I've got to go out and get more for the weekend. I'll be out till dark. You wanna come, Evan?"

Before Evan could answer, Tim said, "I'd like to come very much, Alex. How about if I pack a supper for all of us and we can get going? You can have whatever I catch."

"Me too?" Erica begged.

"We'll be gone a long time, Peanut."

"I can do it, honest. I'll take some comics. I promise I won't complain once. There's nothing to do around here."

Tim looked at Mother. "That's true. But you'd better ask Alex first."

Poor Alex looked trapped. "Sure...uh...I guess so. How about you, Lizzie?"

Evan scowled and muttered. "Count me out. I don't fish in gangs."

"I think I'll hang around here with Gran this afternoon," I said. "Maybe go for a walk. How about it, Gran?"

She looked pleased. "Sounds good. How about you, Connie?"

"What is this?" sneered Evan. "Life at the McGill resort? Are you all little social directors?"

Mother ignored him. "I've got work to do. All of you go and do your little things," she said tersely. "As we won't be going home for a few days, I've got to get some work off to my colleagues. I can't waste time doing nothing."

So Tim had won round two. They were staying for awhile. Round one had been getting her here in the first place. Pretty soon, though, she'd make her move. Tim could end up mincemeat in round three.

Gran and I walked along the long shore path that ended up on a rocky ridge overlooking a wide open stretch of the lake. We sat down on the edge of the ridge and gazed out over the glittering lake.

"Gran?"

"Mmmm?"

"Did you know that someone lived on Rain Island once?"

She was silent for a moment, contemplating the far shore. "How did you discover that, honey?"

"I've been kind of exploring it. For something to do. There's part of an old cabin there. Do you know whose it was?"

She glared at me. "I thought I told you kids to stay away from there. The underwater rocks are treacherous."

"I'm old enough," I said. "I'll be sixteen soon."

"Six months into your fifteenth and already you're sixteen, eh?" She looked out over the lake, thinking. "Still, I guess you're right. You're old enough."

"So, who lived there?"

"Well," she said, leaning back on her hands. "People around here don't know too much about her, you see. She was kind of a mystery woman."

"Her?" I asked in amazement. "You mean a woman lived there?"

She nodded. "Her name was Frances Rain. She moved up here around 1911 or '12, or thereabouts."

I scrambled to my knees. "But why did she live on the island? Was she a prospector? Did she live alone? What did she look like? When did she die?"

Gran laughed and poked me. "Too many questions. She was from Alberta somewhere and she moved up here to be a teacher in The Pas. That was when there was a big rush of mining going on. In the summer she prospected. I don't suppose there's anyone left around here who remembers her...." She looked as if she was going to add something, but then said, "Funny, all she ever wanted was her privacy. She succeeded too well, maybe."

"How do you know? Did you know her? How come you never told me about her before?"

"She died before I moved up here to live for good," she said. "But no one really knew her." She gazed in the direction of the island. "She died there one winter night. Alone. She was still a young woman. Close to your mother's age."

"You sound like you knew her," I said, but she wasn't listening. "Gran? You okay?"

"What? Oh, yes. I'm okay. Well, enough of that." She slapped her hands on her knees and struggled to her feet. "I'm hungry, kiddo. Let's go get something to eat."

I tried to get her to tell me more on the walk home, but she kept pointing out wild flowers and bird sounds, finally distracting me completely.

Mother and Evan had already eaten and were hidden away in their rooms. The sweet sad sound of the flute accompanied our meat and pickle sandwiches and iced tea. The music made me think of Frances, dying alone on the island. Had I seen her hand hovering in front of the door yesterday? It all seemed centuries ago that it had happened.

"I wish you knew more about her," I said.

"Who?"

"The lady of the island. Frances Rain."

"All I know is that everyone who met her said all she ever wanted was to be left alone."

"Sort of like a hermit. Hey, maybe she was running from the law!"

"You do have a busy little mind, don't you, kiddo? Sometimes it's best not to pry. Some things are best left alone, kept in your heart, away from...interference." She stood up.

I looked at her and forgot Frances Rain. "Are you okay, Gran?" Her skin had a dusky greyness behind it.

"I'm fine. Just winded. Your ma and all this nonsense has worn me right out today. Could you do the dishes?" Before I could answer, she added huffily, "And don't go thinking I'm an old crock!"

I put my arms around her. She gripped my shoulders and pressed her lips hard to my forehead.

"Been a long time since anyone did that, Lizzie. I miss it. I miss your granddad. He was quite a hugger. I didn't have too many hugs when I was a kid, but he sure made up for it." She tapped my chin with a long finger. "Now, here I am getting all sloppy. I'm off to bed."

After I did the dishes, I sat on the veranda and thought about Gran. I knew she'd been brought up by her grandparents, but she never talked about her mother and father. She'd been married to Granddad for over forty years, and she'd really loved him. What had it been like to find herself alone? Did Mother feel the same way when Dad left? I hadn't really thought about it that way. Maybe it was even worse when someone left you. Gran's parents had left her. Dad left Mother. Did Frances Rain leave someone behind in Alberta? A whole lot of people had been left behind, it seemed to me.

# CHAPTER SIXTEEN

I TOOK my sketchbook and pencils and sat back down in the veranda. I tried to sketch what I'd seen on Rain Island. Sometimes, when I've transferred something onto paper, I understand a lot more about it. Not this time, though. I held up my pencil drawing of the small cabin. I still couldn't understand where it came from.

If that had been Frances Rain's hand I saw, then why me? Why did I see it? Looking closely at the soft, blurry cabin, I suddenly felt a strange ache deep inside. It's hard to explain, but it was as if the cabin was changing me, as if I was growing outside of me — growing into someone else — someone different and lonely and sad. I slammed the book shut. The feeling disappeared.

I stood up and paced the veranda. Was I going stark raving nuts? Who was this Frances Rain and how could my own drawing give me the willies? *Who was Frances Rain*?

I sat down. She was a teacher and prospector, Gran said. I'd read enough to know that prospecting was no sissy occupation. There were hard climbs through rocky hills, tough slogging through wet muskeg and hordes of blackflies and mosquitoes. There would be long hours spent hammering away at rocks in the high bush country. Then back to her little castle and moat.

Had she chosen to live her life the way she'd wanted, or had she been running away? I thought about Dad. Which one had he been doing?

Here I go again, I thought. Questions and no answers. I can't even answer why my own father left two years ago. How could I possibly find out why Frances Rain came here all those years ago?

All I knew was that I'd live my life the way I wanted, too. And I wouldn't leave anyone behind. Because I wouldn't get married. I'd become a writer or artist. Definitely *not* an archaeologist. Feeling good about my mature decision, I watched the sun go down. Pink and orange edged clouds drifted above the cabin and lit the veranda with a warm glow. The low putt-putt of a small boat moved across my line of vision. Alex angled the boat towards shore. Tim lumbered onto the dock and held the boat while Erica scrambled out, batting mosquitoes with her hat. The three of them swatted bugs, talking and laughing. They stampeded up the path and crowded onto the steps trying to escape the vampire horde.

"Hey, Lizzie," said Erica, "guess how many I caught? Six! Big ones." She held her arms wide apart.

They argued for awhile about who caught the biggest.

"We'll fight this out in the morning, little one," said Tim. "Right now, your eyes are at half mast. Bed!"

Erica was too tired to fight it. She mumbled something about a zillion pound pickerel and wandered sleepily out of the room. Tim sank into one of the big chairs. I expected Alex to make up some excuse to go home, but he sat down beside me. I was glad that it was dark enough to hide the stupid grin on my face. We settled back and looked out over the dusky lake. Bugs tapped and hummed against the screens.

"Do either of you believe in ghosts?" Tim asked, casually.

"Ghosts?" we repeated in unison. Only in my case, it kind of croaked out.

"Not ghosts necessarily," said Tim, "but something paraphysical or otherworldly, if you like."

Alex stared at him. "Why are you asking us? Planning on a good ghost story?"

"No. It's just that...well...the funniest thing happened when we were out on the lake," said Tim. "I've always been a bit — what the Scots call 'fey.' My grandmother was a Scot and she knew when something was going to happen. I can't do that, but I've been into a few houses where I felt...something. A kind of pressure. Anxiety. And a few times, I've been told that the house was thought to be haunted."

"A pressure?" I gasped. "Like when someone pushes on you?"

"A bit like that. But as soon as I leave, the feeling just goes, and I usually convince myself that I ate too many onions for dinner or drank too many beers. Speaking of beers." He got up.

"Wait a minute," I demanded. "You can't just leave. What happened on the lake?"

"Yeah." Alex leaned forward. "That's dirty. Tell us."

Tim fell back on his chair and laughed. "Tell you so you can jeer at me and make fun, huh?"

"No," I said. "Honest. Come on. Give."

"You'll be disappointed, kiddo."

"If you don't tell me, I'll tell Mother that you're dying to go back to the city tomorrow."

He guffawed. "Anything but that! Jeez! You'd make a good interrogator. Get 'im where it hurts. Okay, what happened was this. We were just on our way back and we were passing that big island...the one over there...you can almost see it from here."

I felt my scalp prickle.

"We putted around it, trying for that one last bite, eh, Alex? Well, that's when I felt that pressure I was telling you about. And when I looked over at the island, I thought I saw someone standing on the rock jutting out from it on the far side. But then Erica got her line tangled in mine, and when I looked back, I didn't see anything."

"That's when you asked me if there was a cabin

94

on the island," said Alex. "I wondered why you asked that."

Tim nodded. "But even while you were telling me that no one lived on the place, I saw a light flicker in amongst the trees."

Alex laughed. "You told me you needed a leak, and would I drop you off for a second."

"I couldn't very well tell you that I wanted to check out ghosts, could I?"

I heard my own voice in the distance. "Did you land?"

He nodded. "I just walked a little way up this slope, but I could see there wasn't a cabin anywhere. And there definitely wasn't any light. The mosquitoes drove me back to the boat. Anyway, we circled the entire island afterwards and there wasn't even a canoe pulled up anywhere. But I'll tell you this. The whole time I was on that island, I felt an unearthly sadness all around me." He sat back. "Now call me a fool."

"This person you thought you saw," I asked, trying to sound casual. "Could you make him out? Was it a man or a woman?"

He thought for a minute. "You know, now that I think of it, I would have said it was a woman... no...I couldn't be sure. All I really saw was a sort of flicker." He smeared his hand all over his face and pulled his beard. "I don't know. Probably imagined the whole thing." He grinned sheepishly.

"Weird," said Alex. "Definitely weird."

"I told you you'd start calling me names," chuckled Tim.

95

"Oh, I didn't mean...."

"It's okay, Alex," said Tim, flashing his sugar cubes in the air. "Now, may I get that beer? See you later, kids."

"You didn't tell me your mother had married a madman," said Alex, when he'd gone. I knew he was only kidding, but I guess I was pretty edgy by this time.

"How do you know what he saw or didn't see? You really think he would have told us if he hadn't seen something? You're just like Evan. Think you know everything."

"I was only — "

"It took a lot of guts to tell us that story. If it happened to me, I wouldn't tell anyone. And lots of people — important, intelligent people — have seen ghosts!"

He jumped to his feet. "Hey! Cool down. I was only kidding. If Tim says he saw a ghost, he saw a ghost. Don't get crazy." He shook his head.

"Oh, so now I'm crazy...."

"Will you get serious? How come you're so worked up all of a sudden? You'd think you'd seen a ghost, not Tim."

"And if I had, you'd be making fun of me! Loonie Lizzie, maybe?"

I was acting stupid, but I couldn't seem to stop myself. Acting stupid is like a virus — comes on you without warning.

He held up both hands. "I believe him, okay?" He began to walk backwards to the door. "Look,

I'm not looking for a hit in the nose. Besides, May will be wondering where I am."

I came to my senses too late. "Listen, Alex...I'm sorry. I don't know why I'm jumping down your throat. Everyone around here is tense right now, okay?"

"No kidding. But, no big deal, eh?" He was still backing away. "I gotta go or May'll have my head. I'll see you around, eh?" He took the steps two at a time.

"How about fishing again?" I called.

"Right. Sure. See you around," he said, stiff back and all.

Feeling like a number one hysterical schmuck, I watched the little red and green lights on his boat move across the water. Between Evan and me, we'd done a good job of getting rid of Alex Bird. He'd never talk to me again. He probably thought I was really nuts. I should have told him. But how could I? "By the way, Alex, I not only saw the ghost Tim saw, but the house she lived in." Great. Loonie Lizzie.

Somehow, I had to resolve the mystery of Frances Rain. For a long time, I stood on the veranda and stared over the flat silver bay. In the distance, the island was etched darkly against the navy sky, and I knew that under those distant trees, the golden spectacles were waiting for me.

# CHAPTER SEVENTEEN

I WAS up and out at dawn. After leaving a scribbled note for Gran, I tiptoed down the stairs into a heavy wet mist. The bushes and trees loomed out of the fog, not a breath of air stirring their branches. I'd gone fishing lots of times in thick mist, and the lake on mornings like this was as flat as an antiqued mirror.

I lowered the Beetle into the water and wiped off the cold dew on the seats. Through a spot of thinning mist, a small section of hazelnut bush quivered suddenly and I heard the chink of tiny coins in a warbler's pocket. Someone was up besides me.

I pushed off from shore, my clothes stinking from the mosquito repellent I'd sprayed all over them. This time I'd brought my sketchbook along with my lunch, my bathing suit and a small tape recorder.

The silent mist smothered the Beetle and me with its damp breath. I heard Bram's thin yelp from the veranda, but I couldn't bring him in case he messed up my experiment. Because that's what I was going to do. View the whole thing as a scientific experiment: taking notes on my tape recorder and making sketches. If I'd had a camera I would have brought it. Evan, the rat, refused to lend me his and Tim had an expensive Pentax, which looked like it needed a consulting engineer to travel with it.

Shafts of sunlight, rising above the trees, cut through the fog and soon I was travelling under a layer of disappearing mist. I docked easily and pulled the canoe up onto a grassy ledge.

Clear daylight came to the island like a window shade steadily opening. It hit my shoulders where I sat leaning against an old pine, warming me through my heavy sweater. Time for action.

Working up my nerve, I crept towards the campsite. The spectacles were right where they'd fallen two days ago. I grabbed them, ran back to the old pine near the shore and carefully cleaned them with a soft cloth I'd brought along. From where I was sitting I could just make out the green hump of the cabin's remains.

"I've decided to record everything I see," I said into the little holes of the tape machine. I felt a little silly but who was here to see me? "I am now going to place the glasses on my face...well, on my nose...that is...put them on." I cleared my throat. "I am going to put them on...now."

The visions came quickly. The path appeared just to my right, the cabin straight ahead. I looked towards the shore, and my heart did a flip flop.

A small dock, its stringers lying well up on the

rocky shore, appeared before my eyes, but I could still see the Beetle behind a thickish film. There were two canoes tied to the dock — one a big freighter, the other a small Peterborough, like the Beetle. I tried to describe what I saw without babbling.

The cabin stood low and silvery in the early morning sun. Long-ago leaves danced their shadows across the green roof. When I listened to the tape later, I was surprised at how matter-of-fact I sounded — that is, until all hell broke loose. Figuratively speaking, of course.

"The cabin door seems to be slightly open," I heard myself say, sounding a little like a CBC news correspondent. "As I look around me, it's a clear spring day. Some of the trees are just budding. I wish...uh...uh, wait. There seems to be...there seems ...what? The door is opening...in front of me!"

I can laugh now, but at the time, it was like being kicked in the chest. Every muscle went into rigor mortis. The door was opening all right. I waited, my mouth hanging open. Then it shut. The door, that is.

"I don't see anyone," I said in a strangled whisper. "Whoever closed it must still be in the cabin...wait...I see...I see, I see something moving...uh...it's a person. I think. I can barely see them...him...I can see suspenders, clear as a bell...now trousers — grey I think, and black, thick hair. It's a woman! She's looking towards the lake. Towards me?"

She grew clearer and clearer, almost like a Polaroid picture developing. I felt as if I was talking through a throat that someone's hands were squeezing shut.

"She's turning...going back into the cabin. Wait. Now she's back with a pair of binoculars. It must be Frances Rain. It has to be. Omigod! What am I seeing? I'm seeing a ghost. I don't believe it!" I ran out of breath.

The woman looked through the binoculars at the lake, and I saw her lips move. Then she shook her head and lowered the glasses. She seemed pretty tall. She had wide shoulders, but was slim in the legs and hips. Her skin was darkly tanned and her clothes were rough looking, the shirt rolled up at the sleeves, the high laced hunting boots scuffed right up to the knees.

Gulping, I continued, my voice rasping out the words. "She's turning...she's looking this way...." Silence for at least a minute while I debated what I was going to do if she came my way, then, "Now she's walking...looking...coming... TOWARDS ME!"

All you can hear on the tape after that is a couple of seconds of a rustling sound followed by a few loud clunks when the recorder hit against some rocks. Brave reporter. Miss nothing. That's me. I'd thrown myself on the ground behind some bushes.

From down amongst the twigs and dirt, I saw her legs and booted feet silently pass close by me along the path. One of her laces had a couple of knots in it, I noticed, and one trouser leg was patched at the knee with a lighter fabric.

Stranger yet was that, at the same time, I could actually see the dim outline of the background trees. My trees or hers, I wondered? It gave me a jolt. I could see her so clearly, yet see through her at the same time.

I lay there until I caught my breath, finally crawling to my knees and peering over a low bush. I saw a boat, with two paddlers and two seated passengers, out on the lake. It was a freighter canoe. The crackled grey hull cut deeply through the smooth spring waters, moving rapidly towards the woman waiting on shore.

# CHAPTER EIGHTEEN

I PUSHED my hair out of my eyes and walked around to the path, keeping a sharp eye on the woman just in case she spotted me. I followed the path until I was about ten feet from the shore. Just to be on the safe side, I hid behind the trunk of a wide jack pine. Would she be able to hear my voice, I wondered, turning the tape recorder on again.

"Ahem!" I said loudly. "Ahem, ahem."

No reponse. So I described the people in the canoe.

"The two men paddling have dark skin and braided hair and are wearing identical blue and white plaid shirts," I whispered loudly.

As they moved closer, I realized they were, in fact, twins. They sat unsmiling at either end of the canoe. The man at the back slid his paddle tight against the side of the canoe while the other one rested his across the gunwale. The steerer brought the canoe neatly up to the dock. It slid to a stop, seeming to pass through my own little Beetle at the same time.

Now I was able to see the two passengers on the floor of the canoe — a man and a girl. He was big and wide, dressed in a black coat and wide-brimmed hat. He tried to stand up, making the canoe wobble. The guide at the rear pointed at the floor and said something. The girl clutched at each gunwale and closed her eyes.

The man sat down again, but I knew from the angry movements of his jaw and his jabbing finger that he was not happy with the orders. The guide looked straight ahead, ignoring the lethal finger. I had the feeling that he'd heard it all before.

The girl kept her eyes closed until the canoe stopped rocking. She opened them again when Frances stepped onto the dock. The girl gazed up at her shyly, eyes squinting against the sun. The man in black looked up, too, and I saw his face clearly for the first time. It had a flabby chin that hung from ear to ear. His close-set eyes looked like two pushed-in eyes on a flat potato. His nose was a small smudged thing, but his mouth was like a frog's — a wide moist slit.

I shuddered when I saw it. The look he gave Frances should have knocked her over, but it didn't. She even offered him a hand up.

He ignored her hand and sat where he was, staring at her. She shrugged and walked by, stopping to speak to the guides. The paddler in front hopped out and held the canoe steady.

The Toad Man stepped heavily onto the dock. He was big all right, even taller than he looked sitting down, and really wide, with rounded shoulders under the dark overcoat and the huge fur collar. He took off his hat. The scalp underneath was flat and freckled and edged with a thin fringe of white hair.

I dived behind a tree as his nasty gaze swept the island. When I worked up my nerve to look again, the girl was out of the canoe. She was very thin and wore a long maroon coat and matching bonnet, trimmed with silver buttons. The skinny ankles underneath ended in a pair of thick-soled shoes.

Frances led the way onto shore. Only the two guides stayed back, the steerer sitting in the canoe, his brother crouching on the dock, his arms resting on his knees.

The girl looked around the island with interest. She was about thirteen or fourteen, her face pale and narrow with a big pointed nose reddened with cold. Not pretty. I almost felt sorry for her, but there was something in that face that made me think underneath the pale skin and shyness there was a pretty determined person. I think it was the steady gaze of those dark blue eyes. I liked the look of her.

I was busy describing everything, when she did something that shocked me right down to my sneakered soles. She put her hand in her coat pocket, brought out a pair of gold-rimmed spectacles and put them on. My spectacles!

I was so stunned that it took me a second or two to realized that she was watching Frances and the big man arguing, their arms flying in all directions. Standing there, threatening each other with fierce faces, they suddenly looked a lot alike.

The man kept pushing three fingers in front of Frances's face and she kept leaning back, pushing them angrily away, shaking her head. I watched his mouth form the words, "Three months and no more." Was this how long the girl was going to stay? Was he staying, too? What was going on?

The girl looked for support from the two solemn-faced Indians, but they'd suddenly found their moccasined feet fascinating. When she pushed herself between the two angry people, they both edged her aside.

As suddenly as it began, the argument stopped. Just like that. Frances nodded at the old man and he turned away. The guides looked at each other and shrugged. The girl slumped down on a rock by the shore, staring dismally over the water, her back to the others.

The big man, his face as black as thunder, plodded heavily up to the girl. To my surprise, the hard flat face softened for just one second when he looked down at her bent head, the frog's mouth working as if he were about to speak. When her chin tilted up, the hard look washed back over his ugly face. He spoke with short sharp gestures, holding up his three fingers again, then stomped back to the dock and got into the canoe.

The girl took two or three steps in his direction, one hand outstretched. He took no notice of her. Finally, she dropped her shoulders and waited silently for him to leave.

The twins removed two small boxes and a suitcase tied with a big leather strap from the canoe and placed them carefully on the dock, nodding shyly to Frances. The one on the dock stepped down into the canoe. We watched it move slowly and steadily away. The Toad Man didn't look back once.

Abruptly, Frances turned and with long strides began to walk back up the path to the cabin. She was almost level with me when she hesitated and said something over her shoulder to the girl, who was still standing by the shore, shifting from one large foot to the other. Frances spoke again and the girl turned and picked up her luggage.

I continued to mumble into the recorder, wanting to describe everything I saw, but I felt uneasy with Frances so close. I had this weird sensation of watching a huge, dim television set. Maybe these people weren't even ghosts. Maybe I was peering through a warp in time, looking through a clouded window into the past.

"The sun is glinting off Frances's hair. I can see strands of silver in it. She's that close! She's slim, but she looks as strong as a man. The girl's coming closer. They both look nervous. It's like they've just met. The girl looks anorexic. I wonder if she's been sick. Maybe that's why she's here. A rest cure or something. Funny, the girl's hard to make out; she keeps fading. Frances is as clear as a bell."

Frances's hand lifted, hesitated and touched the girl's shoulder lightly. It was then that I saw the signet ring.

"Hey! That ring. It *was* you I bumped into!" I called out in a loud voice.

She'd heard me.

I could feel a tingle rush down my arms and legs and through my body. She twisted her head sharply to look in my direction. I stood like an idiot gaping at her. Did she see me, too? She blinked rapidly, tilting her head to one side. A brown hand came up to shade her eyes — eyes of piercing blue that seemed to hold me to the spot. Too terrified to move, I looked at the girl, but she was gazing around searching for whatever had caught Frances's attention.

I stepped back, looking down to make sure that I didn't trip over anything. It wouldn't have mattered because my feet weren't there. Or my arms — or my legs. I wasn't anywhere to be seen.

Frantically I searched for myself. I felt around but couldn't see my hands feeling my body, although I felt a faint pricking of pins and needles at each spot I touched. Horrified, I looked up and saw the same amazement in Frances's eyes. I felt for the glasses and in one hard pull they were off. As I lay in a heap, waiting for the roller coaster to grind to a halt, one thing kept pounding in my head. She saw me. Frances Rain saw me.

# CHAPTER NINETEEN

I CLIMBED into the canoe and backpaddled away from the landing rock, my arms and legs on automatic. Only when I'd reached what I considered a safe distance away, did I look back. Rain Island sat there just like normal, cooling its feet in the clear green water around it. I was finally beginning to feel the knots in my back unwind, when something flickered at the edge of my eye.

I felt my eyeballs swell. A small boat was drifting around the edge of the island. An arm lifted and waved in the distance, beckoning, summoning, the water dripping off the oars in silver-threaded beads. Was she coming after me? I swivelled in my seat and paddled hard for home. The Beetle weaved across the bay, like a drunk driver in a go-kart. I heard the creak of oars behind me, coming hard at my back.

"Hey! Stringbean! Slow down!"

Alex's voice came through the roaring of my ears. Real terror makes you deaf, I've discovered.

I stared at the boat streaming up behind me.

When I saw who it was, I slid off the seat and banged my knees on the Beetle's ribs. I let out a couple of lumberjack curses I didn't even know I knew.

"Hey, hold it!" he said, laughing. "Where did you learn words like that?"

"I don't know." I looked around for the culprit.

"Your gran would wash your mouth out with coal oil, not plain old soap, if she heard you right now." He brought the boat a little closer. "You okay, Lizzie? You look like you've seen a ghost." He propped one dripping oar onto the side of the boat.

I shook my head and managed a shaky smile. If only he knew.

"It's okay," I said, "I forgot my watch and I wasn't sure how late it was. I didn't want Tim out trying to rescue me again."

"Tim? Rescue you? When?"

I told him about my adventure in the storm. Talking made me feel better. When he started to laugh loudly, I felt the tension oozing away.

I guess I was staring because he stopped laughing and we looked at each other, and then we both looked away at the same time. Maybe I was going crazy. Nothing seemed normal any more.

"What the heck were you doing on Rain Island, and how come you were paddling away like wolves were after you?" he asked, fiddling with the oarlock.

"Please don't tell Evan I was there, or he'll come over and push his way in and ruin everything."

"Ruin everything? Like what?"

I hesitated, then decided to trust him. Only so far, though.

"Have you ever heard about Frances Rain? The one the island's named after?"

"Yeah, I've heard she lived on the island. She died years ago."

"Do you know anyone who might remember her?"

He shrugged. "Nah. Well...maybe old Harvey might."

"Well, I've been digging around her cabin site. Looking for keepsakes. I thought I might find out more about her." I leaned forward. "And you know what? She had a table with blue dots and tulips all over it. And I'm pretty sure she sat at it looking out a window." That sounded dumb. "I mean, she looked over this very bay. It makes her seem so...real...you know?" I shivered.

He frowned and shook his head, then stared at the island. "Hey, maybe that's who Tim saw last night. The Ghost of Frances Rain."

I smiled weakly. "Maybe he did."

"If she's still around, how do you know she doesn't hate you digging around her place?" he asked.

We were both staring at the island now.

"Alex?"

"Mmmm?"

"Why do you think she might not like it? Are you serious?"

"Well, after Tim told us about seeing something,

and after I left you last night," here he gave me a look through narrowed eyes, "I got to remembering when I came to the island to pick cranberries with May on the east shore. I was just a kid. May told me that some lady had lived there, and she acted kind of funny about it. I remember we talked in whispers and she wouldn't let me go to the middle of the island. The only reason she'd come was because it was a dry year and the cranberries weren't any good, and she knew that Rain Island had good ones no matter what. When we left, she said something about it not being worth it."

"The middle of the island is where the cabin is. Or was. Do you think maybe Tim saw her ghost last night?"

He shrugged. "Ghosts? I don't know. I know that May says there's a spirit in everyone. Once she said that if a person hasn't finished something important when they die, sometimes the spirit stays close by until they get the job done."

I felt the hair rise along my neck. Did Frances have a job to do? Did the girl? And where did I come in to this?

Alex wasn't too concerned about ghosts, obviously, because he changed topics in midstream.

"By the way, I was on my way to your place when my motor conked out. I'm supposed to ask you if you want to come over tonight for blueberry pie and a game of backgammon with May. She figured you'd be ready to come over by now, so she made you her first pies of the season. Fresh this morning." He sounded almost eager, and I guess he heard it too because he shrugged and said, "It's up to you. Makes no difference to me."

"Okay. Sounds good. Will you pick me up?"

"Yeah. I gotta get Harv too. He gets worked up if he misses out on May's first blueberry pie."

"Okay."

"Well, I guess I'd better get a move on," he said.

"Yeah. Okay."

But he kept hanging on to the canoe.

"So did you find anything to bring home from your dig?"

"No. I...." Suddenly I remembered what I'd left behind. "Oh no! I forgot my tape recorder and my sketchbook and...and...."

"Where?"

"On the island. I can't go back," I cried. "I've gotta go back. Oh no!"

"You sound like your tape recorder got stuck in rewind," he laughed.

"I left everything...you know...when I saw...it was...I've got to get my stuff. What if it rains? No, I'll leave it. But I can't." I felt like pulling my hair out. I began to backpaddle away but he held on.

"Did something scare you off the island? Is that it?"

"I've got to get back," I said, poking at the edge of his boat with my paddle. "Let go! I've got to...."

Still he hung on. "I'll take you. We've drifted halfway down the lake. You'll have a heck of a time paddling into this wind."

"I can do it. I've done it all my life. I know how

to get around in a canoe, even if I am a dumb city person,'' I snapped. ''Let go, okay? Just let go.''

''Have it your way. Just wanted to help,'' he snapped back. ''You're running a close neck-and-neck race with Evan for pill of the year. I don't know why I bother with you.''

He let go of the canoe and gave it a little push. A gust of wind turned me around on a dime. I chewed my lip and stared at the now distant island. I couldn't do it alone.

# CHAPTER TWENTY

"ALEX?"

"Yeah?"

"If you have time, I guess I'd like that tow to the island." I had to shout the last part as the wind carried me along.

"I got time, I guess. City slicker."

He pulled close and we grinned at each other. I climbed into the boat while he tied the Beetle's rope to the oarlock. The island was bathed in the warm afternoon sunlight. I sat on the tip of the bow, my feet dragging in the water, while he rowed. When we reached the island, I stuck my foot out to keep the boat from crunching into the landing rock, and for just a second was surprised not to see Frances's dock. I shook my head. It was getting harder and harder to figure out what I was really seeing. Alex walked up the flat slope.

"Coming?"

I stood rooted to the landing rock and nodded. In the distance I heard the sad cry of a loon. Alex walked back and stood in front of me. His long fingers wrapped around my chin and moved my head from side to side. I looked up.

"Good. At least you're not catatonic. Blink," he demanded. I blinked. "Good, good. Now open your mouth and say something."

"Will you help me collect my stuff?" I croaked.

"Good. Voice still functioning. What did you see here? A bear?"

I shook my head.

"A snake?"

I sneered and shook my head.

"Oh, yeah, I forgot. You used to collect them. There's only one thing left. Persons living or dead?"

I nodded, then slumped down on the rock. He crouched beside me, arms resting on his knees.

"Is it this ghost of Tim's?"

I nodded again.

"A ghost? For real? Where?"

"I saw her at the cabin site, at the dock, on the path," I said softly.

"Who?"

"Her. Them."

"Her. You mean this Frances Rain person?"

"I think so." I felt the tightness in my throat start to loosen. "It's happened twice. Two days ago and today."

"So that's why you acted so mad last night."

I nodded. "And today, when the cabin door opened and she...."

"Wait a second. Cabin doors opening? I've passed by this island lots of times, Lizzie. I hate to tell you this but there are no cabins on this island. Not any more at least."

"Well, there's one in the middle of the island. Where your aunt wouldn't take you. Just a few logs left. But I saw all of it when I saw her. The whole thing was standing there."

"You saw the ghost of a cabin? In the flesh? I mean, in the wood?"

"Do you want to hear this or just kid around?"

"I'm all ears. Honest."

"Okay. This is what I saw. I saw a cabin and five people. The guides don't really count 'cause they didn't do much. They were twins. Did you ever hear of twin Indian guides in the area?" I looked at him looking at me. "You don't believe me, do you?"

"Yes. Believe it or not, I do. And are you lucky or what? What an incredible experience. What was it like? How did you feel? Never mind, I can tell. Did anyone tell you you don't suit pale green? Especially around the gills."

"You really do believe me?"

"Sure, why not? You've never made up stories. If anything, you always tell things pretty straight out. That's why you acted so weird last night. You couldn't tell it like it was, without running the risk of looking nutty. Besides, no one could look like they've seen a ghost more than you do. Correction...ghosts." He grinned. "You're just not the wild and crazy kind, Stringbean."

"No, I'm not the wild and crazy kind. I'm just plain old boring Lizzie. No imagination, dull, boring Lizzie, that's me."

He stood up. "I didn't mean that. I just meant that you're not...you know...crazy. Hysterical. Nutso!" He was getting louder. "I don't even know what we're talking about half the time any more. I say something and you jump all over me."

I put my head down on my knees. He was right. I wasn't making any sense. Nothing made any sense. "You want to hear something really crazy?" I said to my knees. "I mean, *really* crazy?"

"Sure," he said, sitting down again.

"The crazy thing is I know I'll put the glasses on again. I want to see more."

"Glasses? What glasses? Maybe you'd better start at the beginning. Step by step."

I went over the events again slowly, as much to set it clearer in my mind as to tell Alex. When I was finished, I lifted my head and looked at him. He was lying on his back, his arms above his head, long legs stretched out, black eyes watching me.

"Still think I'm not nuts, Alex?"

He gave that some long serious thought. I hit him in the stomach. "Hey! That hurt." But he was laughing.

"Well?"

"I never said you were normal, I said you weren't crazy. If you were normal, you'd be dull, unimaginative and boring!"

It felt good to laugh. Suddenly he was on his feet, pulling me with him. His hands were hard and dry. And the rest was flesh-and-blood real. No ghost there. He pulled me towards the trees.

"Let's collect this stuff of yours and look around."

He walked through the flickering light towards the dreaded spot and I forced myself not to call out a warning. When I got there, he was standing over my dig, hands on hips.

"Great place for a cabin, eh? I'd love to live here. It feels...special."

I nodded. With Alex beside me I was almost able to enjoy the cool green stillness again.

"Would you help me put the tabletop and all the other stuff back again?" I asked. "And the moss?"

"Not going to dig around any more?" he asked.

"Maybe later," I said. "Right now, I want to sort out what happened to me here."

He nodded. It took us awhile to put everything back, but when we were through only the dark outlines around the moss patches showed that anyone had been mucking around.

"Where's the glasses?" he asked.

"In my pocket."

"Put them on now. While I'm here."

"Are you nuts?" I backed away.

"Let me try them then." He put out a hand.

I had to laugh out loud when he put them on. "You look like an old-fashioned bank clerk. All you need is a stiff collar and cuffs."

"Thanks. A dull and boring clerk? How can I get into the spirit of things with you giggling? Spirit of things. Get it?"

I couldn't help a few more snickers at the frowning face behind the silly little glasses. He turned slowly around. Then he pushed them down and looked at me over the rims.

"How long did it take you to see something?"

"Almost right away. The first time the whole place turned to autumn colours. The second time, it was spring. See anything?"

He squinted. "Nothing. Zilch." He took them off. "Zero, darn it. How come you get to see things and I don't?"

" 'Cause you're not crazy."

"Must be that," he said, shaking his head sadly. "Loony Lizzie. Sad story indeed."

I was angry until I saw the wicked smile. "You poor thing. You're just jealous, that's all."

"Come on, now I'm here, you don't have to be afraid."

"But I *am* afraid. Maybe if we stood away from the cabin. Down by the shore. I wouldn't bump into anyone. What do you think?"

"What if you put them on right here, in the middle of the cabin? Maybe you'd be inside it."

"And what if I can't get out?" I shivered.

"Okay, let's move over here. Will you try it?"

"Okay. But only if you stay close by."

He grinned. "My pleasure."

Flustered, I stumbled towards a row of pine, leaned against a tree and put the glasses up to my eyes.

"See anything?"

"No."

"Now?"

All I saw was the sunken site ahead, the cool green light, the pile of gear, and the sparkling lake.

"How about now? Am I here, for instance?"

"Yes, you are. And stop waving your hand in front of my eyes. It makes me dizzy."

He ran to the cabin and waved. "Now? Not even the cabin?"

"Nope." I wasn't sure whether to feel glad or disappointed. I put the glasses in my pocket. "Funny, huh? Maybe I am nutso."

He shrugged. "It's like seances, poltergeists and stuff like that. Bring in another person and nothing happens. Doesn't mean it didn't happen before. Let's go to your place. I'll beg dinner off Terry. We'll think things over on the way to my place. Hey, we could ask Harv about Frances Rain."

"No kidding? That's a great idea. We can pick his brain."

"Picking old Harv's brain may take some doing, but it's worth a try. After dinner, you can use Terry's boat to tow me back to the truck and then you'll have a boat to come back home in. That damn motor of mine is ready for the dust heap."

As we floated away from the island, I couldn't help wondering if I'd ever see Frances again. Maybe the glasses had lost their ability to look into the past. I felt a strange sort of ache at the thought of not seeing her or the girl again.

I needn't have worried. Frances and I had a long way to go.

# CHAPTER TWENTY-ONE

"YOUR family's like a bunch of porcupines," Alex said, bumping his truck around the deepest potholes on the dirt road. "Very prickly. What's with all of you?" When I didn't answer he said, "I mean, who stuffed the lemons in your mother's mouth? It couldn't have been Tim. He spends most of his time acting like it's all his fault and trying to take them out. But she keeps slapping him down. And poor Terry. I think your gran'll be glad to see the back ends of you guys."

I looked out the truck window, only half seeing the trees as they blurred past. He was right. Dinner had been another rotten meal — Mother and Tim silent and grim, Erica tired and weepy, Evan growling over his meat. Gran had looked pretty wiped out by the time dishes were done and hadn't come with us after all, saying she had a headache. I was worried about her.

"She looked pretty tired, didn't she?" I said finally. "I wonder if she's been sick this winter and didn't tell us?"

This time it was his turn not to answer.

"Well, was she? She always writes that she's fine."

He hesitated. "Well...when I was helping her around the place this spring, she seemed out of breath a few times. And she was sort of a funny grey colour."

I felt something squeeze my heart.

"I told Aunt May and she promised to get her in to see Doc Lindstrom. Doc gave her some kind of pills. Don't know what they are, but May said she'd be fine." He gave me a searching glance. "Still if I were you, I'd tell the Munsters over there to let up a little. I don't think she can stand the strain."

That made me mad. "You and May knew my gran was sick and you didn't bother to write? What if she'd got really sick? In the hospital? Would you let her die before telling us? God! You'd think she was your family, not mine!"

"She is like my family. Besides, Terry told us not to tell you," he snapped.

We drove along in black silence for awhile.

The evening sun was pouring orange light into the cab of the truck. I held my hand over my eyes to shade them. It gave me time to gulp down a few self-pitying tears.

"Next time, I'll write. No, I'll call. I promise," he said.

"Thanks," I muttered. "Sorry. I'm always yelling at you."

He grinned. Sunlight warmed his skin to a mellow bronze. "Hey, forget it. I haven't seen your whole family together for ages." He paused. "About your dad. I'm sorry about him leaving. I didn't say anything last year — Evan kept saying he'd probably be leaving for Toronto to stay with your dad for good."

"You can see how that promise came out," I said bitterly.

"Yeah. When I saw Evan this year, I didn't know what to say."

"You? At a loss for words? Spare me."

"Funny."

"Nothing much is funny, really."

"But what's happening anyways?" he asked. "Or am I poking my big schnozz in where it's not wanted?"

I rolled down the window and let the cool breeze whip my hair around my face. I told him everything — how my dad left so suddenly, how we got short cheery notes and big birthday cheques and that was about all. And I told him how Tim had walked into the mess about three months before.

"Does your mother always act like this?"

I shook my head. "She's always been busy, but at least she used to be interested in what we had to tell her, you know? Now, it's like she's walking around on broken bottles. She always seemed so cool and organized."

He nodded. "So she's been acting strange since your dad left?"

"Yeah. But you know what's really weird? She and Dad hardly ever saw each other. I don't think they were...you know...in love, any more. He used to be away for days at a time just before he left. Mother called them business trips, but we knew different.''

"And then he went to Toronto?"

I nodded. "I guess it hurt her a lot. Evan misses him the most. I don't. I guess I'm strange."

He flicked me a quick look. "Do you think she loves old Tim?"

"You know what? I bet she does. She seemed happier when they got married. He's so different from Dad. *He's* always around. He's crazy about her. He used to tease her and make her laugh. That was a new experience, believe me."

"And you? Do you like Tim?"

"I don't know."

"Yes, you do — like him, that is."

"I guess so."

"You should try talking to your mother."

"Are you kidding?" I scoffed.

"No harm in trying."

We rode the rest of the way in silence, but by the time we rolled into Harvey's yard, I'd made up my mind. He was right. There was no harm in trying. At least I'd find out what she was planning on doing about Toothy.

Harvey was waiting in his rocker on the porch of his shack. A gust of wind lifted the edges of its mismatched shingles and swirled the smoke from its chimney into the trees above. Harv rocked two or three times to get enough momentum to pop himself out of the seat and lurched down the dirt path that cut through a yard full of rusting motors, dead and gutted trucks and cars and piles of corroding junk. He pulled his baseball cap out of his pocket and dragged it over the dandelion fluff on his head.

I'd only been inside the shack a few times. All I'd seen were rows and rows of piled magazines, newspapers and books that stretched up to the wood ceiling, with hemp ropes and silky strings of cobwebs holding it all together. Harvey claimed to have read every word of those millions of pages and couldn't bear to part with one of them.

I remember seeing a mouse's head pop out of the middle of one of the dusty piles the first time I was there. He'd looked around with pink eyes before disappearing, probably to get on with his reading.

Alex and I rolled down our windows. It was usually a good idea to have fresh air around when Harvey got into a closed space. His galvanized bathtub, hanging to one side of the front door, rarely got a working out. I shifted closer to Alex to make room. His arm, which had been resting along the back of the seat, dropped around my shoulders. I relaxed against it until Harvey creaked his way into the cab, but then the arm was needed to shift gears.

May greeted us with two huge pies, oozing dark sweet juice. We ate in the kitchen, around the big worktable.

"Say, Harv," Alex said, finally changing the topic from blueberry pies and fishing. "Elizabeth here has been poking around on Rain Island. She found some remains of a cabin. Wasn't that some woman prospector's place?"

Harvey swallowed a slug of coffee, his Adam's apple bobbing up and down his scrawny neck.

"Why that would be Frances Rain's place." He leaned back and picked his teeth. "Haven't thought about her for years."

"Did you meet her?"

"I hung around with a boy whose father owned one of the large silver mines. I'd just come over from the old country. A kid myself. This boy's dad was always after Frances Rain to sell her claim on Pebble Lake, 'bout ten miles straight north of here. Thought she was an amateur at first. But she wasn't no dummy. She'd been trained by Rudy and Pearl Pepin. A better pair of prospectors you'd never find. I guess I musta been about twenty, twenty-one when Frances died. I've made and lost a few fortunes since then, eh, May?"

She laughed and said, "From what I hear, you still got a pile stashed away in that bank in The Pas."

"Well," he said, with a secret smile, "I ain't gonna starve before I die, eh?" And then he chuckled. "Now this Frances Rain you're talking about, she must've made money in her day. Most of us worked with partners. Not her. She was a mystery, that one."

"Do you know where she came from?" I asked.

"I heard she was a teacher in The Pas for a while. She got to know the Pepins and came out prospecting with them. The last ten years or so she stayed out here all year 'round. Built that place of hers with her own two hands. Kept herself to herself. No man dared go near her or she'd of blowed his head right off. The Pepins were her only friends and their base was 'way over on Braid Lake. People said this Frances Rain got a bit queer as time went on." He spun his finger beside his temple. "Nutty."

"Nutty? You mean crazy?" I remembered the black-haired woman I'd seen. She hadn't looked crazy.

"Not all that uncommon around here in them days, my lovely," Harvey said, digging into a fresh piece of pie. "Fortunes lost and found...long dark winters. She was a city girl, I heard. Not used to the loneliness. Course I don't believe she killed herself."

"Killed herself?" I cried.

"So the gossip has it. No, I figure she died of exposure or pneumonia or something. The Pepins found her. Family claimed the body and that was that."

"What family came to get her?" I asked.

"Some big shot out west, if I recall right."

"So you never met her," I said, feeling let down.

"I didn't say that. I just didn't know her, but then no one did. I met her a couple of times, but I only saw her cabin inside the once. Books lining every wall. Don't know how she got them there. Place was full of books."

"You should talk," said May. "One day, I'll clean your place out."

"You do and you'll answer to me," he growled. "No, she told me, that one time, that reading took

128

the place of madness on long freezing days and nights. She was right. She had a whole set of Dickens I'd have given my eye teeth for. 'Cept I didn't have any then, neither. Reading's my only pleasure now. That and blueberry pie.'' May gave him another piece.

''Can you describe her?'' I held my breath and waited.

''Frances Rain? Let's see....Tall. Black-haired. Bony — I like my women with flesh on 'em — and two of the bluest eyes you'll ever see. She had a look about her...it was like she was burning inside with something. Guess that's why people thought she was odd. She made you uncomfortable.''

''I've been on her island a couple of times,'' May said. ''There's a strange empty sadness there, as if it's waiting for someone.''

I took another deep breath. ''Did she ever have a sister, or a niece visit her? A younger girl? Say about thirteen?''

He frowned at the table. ''You know,'' he said, chewing slowly. ''I do recall a little lass visiting her once. A sister, I believe it was. Can't remember exactly.'' He pointed at me with his fork. ''The girl was sickly. Frank Noble over at the company store said that Frances came in now and again for special things for the girl. Said her appetite was poor. Funny you should know about the girl. I'd forgotten all about it. How did you hear of her?''

I shrugged. ''By the way, do you recall a couple of Indian guides from around here at that time? Identical twins?''

He peered at me through his wild eyebrows. "Now, how do you know things I'd forgotten years ago? Sure, they worked around here. The Macdonald twins. Best trappers in the district. You're something, you know that?"

"How long did the girl stay?"

The baseball cap's peak waggled back and forth. "No idea. Summer's prospecting time. No one hung around."

"Did you ever see her?"

"No. Can't say I did. Just heard about her from Frank Noble."

"Do you know when Frances Rain died?"

"Now that I can tell you. Same year as my partner Len and me sold our first big claim. Yep. The year she died, we hit the big time. It was nineteen hundred and twenty-five."

# CHAPTER TWENTY-TWO

I SAT stunned. How had I been able to see a woman who'd been dead for more than sixty years? I'd seen her and she'd seen me. May's clattering in the sink finally woke me up. It was time to help with the dishes.

Alex got up and grabbed a tea towel. I saw him looking at me out of the corner of his eye. "You okay?" he asked quietly.

I nodded.

"Never mind with those dishes, Alex," May said, "I want you to check out the new Evinrude. The Rossmonds over in cabin two are having trouble with it. Would you drain it and put the proper mixture in? He's been using straight gas again."

Alex looked at me and then at May. "Well, that'll take some time."

May cocked her head and looked at me. "Lizzie won't mind, will you, Lizzie?"

I felt a flush creeping up my neck. "Why should I mind?"

"I'll give the kid a hand," said Harvey. "Your

girl will still be here when you're done. Don't you worry none, Alex."

"We're gone," said Alex, backing towards the door. He tripped over the door ledge and out into the night.

"Let's play backgammon, kiddo," May said.

I hate it when adults get secret smiles on their faces.

We played until around eleven o'clock. I was tempted to talk to her about what I'd seen on the island, but I couldn't. It seemed too private to share with a grown-up. She may understand, but then again she could just as easily screw up her wrinkled little face and laugh. I couldn't take that chance.

Alex came in just as we finished a glass of lemonade.

"Let's go," he said. He was covered in grease and not happy. "Don't ever allow those stupid Rossmonds on this land again, or I quit. He won't even admit he used car gas in the damn thing."

"Don't worry," said May. "When I caught their kids stealing chocolate bars from the shelf I figured this was their last wilderness adventure in this lodge. You better get Lizzie home, eh?"

Alex dropped Harv off first. We drove along the moonlit road to Rain Lake in horrible silence. When the truck ground to a halt in front of the trail down to the lake, we sat staring out into dark bushes with silver-edged leaves. The air vibrated with the chirrups of crickets and galumphs of frogs.

"Hope you brought a flashlight," Alex finally

said to the windshield. "You've got a lot of lake to cover."

I leaned against the door of the truck, one hand on the door handle. "I'll be fine. The boat's got running lights. Besides, you can see better at night without a flash."

"You're right. In the daytime, too, I hear."

I smiled out the window. "Won't take me long. Look how quick we made it from Gran's. And I was towing you."

That ended that exciting conversation. I was about to open the door when he said, "So, did you learn anything about Frances Rain from Harvey?"

I shook my head. "But what I did learn was that I really saw her on the island. It was her all right. Harv described her perfectly. And he says there was a girl. And he knew about the Macdonald twins."

"It's really incredible. I wish I could see them. See? You're not loony after all. She must have been an odd one, eh?"

"He says some people thought she was a nut. But I think she was just different. And she was smart. *And* a woman who didn't need a partner to survive in the wild. Put those three together with a cabin on an island and you get some people calling you crazy."

"Was she good looking? Beautiful?"

"Not really. A strong face. But her eyes were blue, blue." I thought a minute. "I guess some people would call her beautiful." I leaned my head back against the seat. "I'm never going to get married either. The way my parents hashed up their time together, I don't see why anyone would bother."

"Next thing you'll be saying is that you're going to live on an island, too."

"Maybe I will. I'll be a famous writer. Or an artist. I'll sell my stuff through your lodge. All those rich Americans. I'd do all right."

"Well, you may not be loony, but you're sure different from any of the girls at school. Maybe you'll be the next Frances Rain. You're different. You're smart. And you're a girl. You're not even bad looking. Better than last year, that's for sure."

"Thanks for the compliment," I said sarcastically. "You don't weigh ten tons any more, so you've improved somewhat, too."

"Yeah. Ken and Barbie."

We both grinned at the windshield.

"Well, I gotta go. Gran'll be worried." I opened the door and stepped down.

He followed me down the path. From the ridge of rock, the bay below looked like molten silver. The mosquitoes that had chased after us were blown away on the breeze off the lake.

"Hey, get a load of the stars, eh?" he said, sitting down on the rock.

I sat down beside him and looked up. The sky was a wide dark cloth covered with silver dots.

"Sorry about my dear Aunt May."

"Why? I had fun."

"You know. About the 'if Lizzie doesn't mind' bit. As if you were my girlfriend or something."

I shrugged. "That's okay."

We sat staring at the stars thinking that one over. At least I was.

"I guess I'd better go," I said, but I didn't move.

He didn't answer. His face came closer and we looked at each other. His eyes came in and I felt my own face shifting closer. The kiss was short. Some might argue that it wasn't a kiss at all. Then what?

"So, I guess I'd better go," I said. I thought I'd already said that. "Okay?"

"Okay."

The next kiss was a little longer and could be seriously judged as a real one. I was surprised our noses didn't get in the way.

We walked hand in hand to the boat, barely aware of the mosquitoes who'd caught up to us in the sheltered lower area. They screamed at us while we kissed one more time, me in the boat and him kneeling on the dock. That time our noses definitely got in the way.

The motor started on the first pull.

"See you," he mumbled.

"Yeah, see you."

I turned the boat around and cranked up the motor. I turned. He waved wildly as the boat skimmed over the moonlit water. I waved just as wildly back.

# CHAPTER TWENTY-THREE

ALEX showed up first thing the next morning, and after that I met him at the landing every day. We spent most of our time at the lodge, helping May during the day and playing backgammon and cards in the old living room at night.

I asked Evan along a couple of times, but he only sneered and said rude things about big noses attracting each other all over the world.

A couple of the days, Alex and I tried to get the ghosts to return to Rain Island, but we had no luck. I figured the spectacles had lost their magic. Then Alex had to go with his dad and a group of Americans on a fishing trip for a few days, and I went back to Rain Island on my own.

Frances and the girl appeared as easily as the picture on my colour TV, and seeing them seemed as natural as seeing reruns of "Star Trek" on Saturday morning.

They didn't stay long that first time back, but at least it was long enough to tell me that the girl was still there. She was lying on an old straw couch outside the cabin door in the dappled shade of the trees. When I edged closer, I saw that she was sketching in pen and ink on the pages of a large sketchbook. Frances was sitting beside her, repairing stretchers for furs. They weren't talking but they looked content enough.

The next day, they were in much the same positions, except Frances was reading a book. Now and again she'd look out over the lake with a strangely longing look. Once, the girl looked up from her work and said something. Frances shook her head. The girl pointed towards the dock. Frances shook her head again. The girl seemed upset. She leaned towards Frances and began to beg. When she started to get up, Frances leaned over and pushed her gently back into the cushions on the couch. Frances nodded and touched the girl's head briefly before walking into the cabin. She came outside a few minutes later with a small backpack over one shoulder. The girl and I watched her push her little canoe into the glaring sunshine. She turned and waved. The girl waved happily back.

When she'd gone a few feet, I raced to the Beetle ready to follow her. But by the time I'd turned the canoe around she was gone.

Each day after that, I returned to watch. Sometimes Frances was there; sometimes it was just the girl and me. I brought my sketchbook and coloured pencils and it was more than weird to sit there sketching someone who was sitting there sketching, and her not knowing I was there — you know what I mean. I think.

Sometimes the images stayed longer and the colours seemed brighter, and once I even thought I heard their voices muffled and distant in my head. Sometimes the glasses would warm to my skin and I'd feel a presence close to me, almost touching but not quite. Who was it standing beside me? The girl? Frances? What did they want me to see? Were they using me like a projector to relive their time together? Were they standing beside me all the time watching with me? Were they trying to tell me something?

On the day that Alex was coming home, something happened but I didn't know at the time what it meant.

When I arrived at the island, I put the glasses on before docking. I floated through their dock, but I felt a hesitation, almost a gentle nudge before I passed through the image. I pulled the canoe on shore and was about to walk up the slope, when the girl appeared, walking towards me.

She was dressed in oversized pants and a plaid shirt. Her hair was a wild mass around her head, and her long nose was peeling and red. She wasn't wearing her glasses. It's silly, I know, but when she walked past me, without seeing me, I felt lonely and unimportant, as if I had just been snubbed.

She seemed so much stronger and healthier now, and after she passed by, I felt that I knew her from somewhere, somewhere other than the island. I shook my head. I could imagine anything now.

I looked around and realized that leaves were turning colour on their side of time. Already? How much time — their time — had passed in the last few days? In one week, I'd only caught bits and pieces of her summer with Frances.

She clambered into the freighter canoe and reached down to hoist a makeshift sail which she put into place by dropping the end of the slender mast through a hole in one of the canoe's thwarts. The wind caught it and pulled her away from shore. She leaned her head back and laughed into the wind that whipped her long brown hair around her head. Did I hear the echo of her laughter through the rush of autumn breezes?

Playing the fool, she stood up and pretended to be looking for other boats, doing a *Pirates of Penzance* stand on the seat. She turned quickly and waved at someone on the shore. I waved back and then realized what I was doing and dropped my hand. I felt someone beside me. Frances walked past onto the dock. She was calling out to the girl and gesturing for her to sit down. The girl just laughed and waved.

The huge canoe floated gently away with the girl waving with great swoops to the lone figure on shore. Frances laughed and waved back, then sat down on the dock cross-legged and watched the girl tack back and forth across the dazzling bay, using her hand as a shade against the strong sun.

A wide grey cloud suddenly scudded across the sun's path, and when she lowered her hand she wasn't laughing anymore. Tears were falling down her cheeks and her face was twisted with sorrow.

Why? Had I missed something? What hadn't the

glasses allowed me to see? What was happening? I felt like screaming with frustration. It couldn't be the girl's illness, not when she looked this healthy. I watched her playing around in the boat. Surely she was getting better.

Then another, more likely idea hit me. What if the girl's visit was coming to an end? What if the Toad Man would be returning soon?

I tried to hold on, wanting to comfort Frances, but first she, then the girl and then the canoe, disappeared into the smoky blue of my own summery world. Whenever the image ended on its own like this, the horrible dizziness and headaches didn't happen, just a fidgety muggy feeling like the one you feel when you wake up from a soggy afternoon nap.

I paddled away from the island, feeling as if I was deserting someone when they really needed me. If only I could have helped her. But how? I shook my head. I was really going crazy. Tell me this. How could I help someone who had been dead for over sixty years?

Before long, I was going to find out.

# CHAPTER TWENTY-FOUR

EVERYTHING was quiet when I got home. Too quiet. Erica and Tim must have been swimming some time in the morning. The old black rubber raft had been pulled up on the sandy strip down by the dock. Sand pails, toy boats and other toys were scattered along the dock and shoreline.

As I walked up the path, I pulled my T-shirt away from my sticky back. The screen door creaked under my touch. Something moved on the lounge by the far window. I saw Erica's spiky hair, pulled into a butterfly clip, poke up from behind the arm of the chair.

"Hi," I said.

She twisted away and looked hard at the hummingbird hovering at the feeder outside the screen. Something in that movement and the damp tendrils of dark hair around the side of her pink cheeks made me stop and take a closer look. She'd been crying.

I pushed her legs over and sat down. "What's up?"

She glared at me. "What do you care?"

"What do you mean by that? I just asked what was up."

"And I said, what do you care?" She brushed her damp hair back with a pudgy hand.

"I care. Is something wrong?"

She shrugged. "Nothing's wrong! Tim's gone. That's all."

"Gone? Where?"

"I don't know. He took his big purple bag and Gran drove him away. He left."

"You mean, he *left*? As in, gone for good?"

"You're stupid as Mama," she said in a dull voice. "I told her the same thing when she got back from her walk. And she asked the same thing. He left her a note. He asked me to give it to her. He said he'd visit me regular. But he won't. Daddy doesn't. But I don't care." Her eyes told me differently.

"Well, you've still got me, you know."

"You don't ever even talk to me any more. You leave every morning and you come back after I'm in bed. I only see you sometimes at dinner and then you only talk to Gran."

"Where is she?"

"I told you! She took Tim over. She isn't back yet. They wouldn't even let me come. She said she was going to the lodge."

"How did she seem? Mad?"

She nodded. "Yeah."

"Where's Mom?"

She shrugged with disgust and muttered, "They

argued for a long time. She told Tim to get lost. She said she was going home and if he didn't like it he could lump it. Is that what lumping it means? Leaving?''

''I guess it does. But don't worry. He'll be back.''

She sat up straight. ''Oh no, he won't, Elizabeth McGill! You and Mama and Evan hate him! He's my best friend. He's the nicest person on earth. And I *hate* the rest of you creeps. Only Gran is okay and she's always been yours, not mine. And you even leave *her* to go out with Alex Bird every day!''

That hit home. All of it hit home. She was right about everything. I hadn't given Gran more than a passing thought. Even worrying about her health hadn't lasted long. I was too busy with Alex or Frances and the girl.

''You're wrong about Tim and me, though,'' I said. ''I like Tim.''

''Oh, yeah? Since when?''

She was right again. I hadn't even bothered to let him know he was okay. And what had happened to the promise I'd made to myself to talk to Mother?

So Tim was gone, thanks to me. And Evan. And Mother. We'd done it together. For different reasons. But we all needed him, I realized with a start. I remembered Frances's tears and how helpless I'd felt not being able to do anything. Here was something maybe I *could* fix.

''I'll get him back somehow. And I'll hang around more. Honest.''

She turned her face into the pillow of the lounge.

143

Promises, promises. She was right. Boy, was I paying. What a mess.

The cabin was quiet. I thought the living room was empty until I saw Evan's head over the top of the couch.

Kicking off my sweaty sneakers, I said, "Where's Mother? I've got to talk to her."

He looked over his shoulder. I heard the clink of ice in his Coke. "How should I know? Outside somewhere. I guess you heard that Sunshine Boy left, huh? Hallelujah."

I sat on the arm of a chair. "Erica told me."

"Stupid jerk didn't last long, did he?" he sneered. "These big guys act tough, but they crumble easy. And to think I wasted my time taking him fishing these past few days."

"You did?"

"So? That doesn't mean we're engaged. He was a pain in the ass, anyway. Now, it looks like I won't have to humiliate him on the raquetball court this winter. He was going to drag me to his club and make me join. He owes me two blue Repella hooks and a rod. He'd better pay up."

I gaped at him. "You mean that you and he were going to join a club together?"

"Don't get me confused with Erica. I just told him I'd go to get the big oaf off my back. I'll be glad when I finally move in with Dad."

"Grow up, Evan. Don't you know yet that Dad isn't going to have you or any of us kids there? It'd hamper his style. Mother got in the way of his act, too. That's why he left."

144

"And why did Tim leave? Eh? Tell me that? Are we in the way of his act?"

"No, I think he left because he was in the way of all *our* acts. He'd never leave the way Dad did."

We looked at each other. I guess we both knew it was true.

"But I'll tell you one thing, Evan. I'm going to straighten this mess out, if it's the last thing I do. Tim will be back. You'll see!"

"I'll see it and then I won't believe it," he said softly.

I walked out of the room, down the hall and out the back door in search of my mother. I, for one, was not going to sit around waiting for something to happen.

# CHAPTER TWENTY-FIVE

I FOUND her sitting on the steep ledge where Gran and I had talked about Frances Rain. She looked around when she heard me coming, and I thought she was going to make a run for it, but then she sighed, slumped forward and looked out at the lake.

A heavy ridge of dark clouds was piling up behind the far shore. Small ochre clouds were being herded ahead while the big ones puffed themselves up and rolled uneasily towards us. Everything seemed dark blue and yellow.

"Storm coming," I said. "Big noisy one from the looks of it."

She shifted to make room for me. I sat down.

"Tim's gone, eh? Erica told me."

She nodded. Her hands on her knees were tightly clenched, the thumbs tucked inside.

"I was just getting used to him," I said. "His leaving was our fault, I guess. Evan and me. We didn't try very hard. Sorry."

She gave me a wry smile. "You two didn't help,

but it was Tim and me...no, I failed Tim." She shivered against the cool breeze that suddenly drifted off the choppy water below. "He tried. I didn't. End of marriage. It wasn't fair to marry him when I wasn't ready. Still, I hoped...." Her words trailed off.

"Why did you marry him?"

"Tim? Don't you think we simply fell in love?"

"Did you?"

"Believe it or not, I think we did. But I've never been really sure why I married him so quickly. Yes — yes, I guess I do know. Because I was scared. Because I was lonely. Because I could see myself getting old without someone who'd finally understand how I was feeling without explanations. I felt like one of those people who stand high above the traffic on a narrow ledge. Tim seemed to be able to keep me from looking down. For awhile."

She seemed to be talking more to herself than to me. I wasn't sure if I should even be listening. Still I had to try.

"Then what went wrong?" I asked in a quiet voice. We'd never talked like this before.

She rested her chin on her knees. "I think I kept expecting him to go inside and close the window and leave me out on the ledge alone."

"Like Dad did?"

She looked at me, surprised. "Yes, like that."

"Tim wouldn't do that."

"But I just couldn't convince myself. So I figured it would be better if I didn't get too close."

"Do you still want to be with him?"

She laughed. It sounded distant and sad. "Yes, I think I do."

"It doesn't have to be over," I offered. "He's nuts about you. Well...realistically, maybe you're second to Erica, but still up there on his list."

She laughed. "No. I'm not sure I'd be on his list now."

"Are you kidding?"

"You wouldn't understand, Elizabeth." Her voice sounded choked off.

"What's to understand? You love him and he loves you. Dad left us because he didn't want to be with us any more. Tim wants to be with us. Cripes! We couldn't get rid of him. You could try at least, couldn't you? It must be worth a try."

She looked up at the rolling clouds. Tears ran out of the corners of her eyes. I waited.

Finally she said, "I guess it's worth a try. It would be...hard. But Tim...."

"But Tim what?"

Mascara had run into the hollows of her eyes. Her hair was all over the place. Was this my mother? "Tim said he was through when he left here," she said. "I have a feeling that he meant it."

"Like they say in the romance novels, Mother, go after him. If Tim saw *you* coming for *him*, he'd know you loved him. And you do, don't you? You said so, didn't you?"

She nodded.

"Then, go and talk to him. Drag him back. And

stay here with us. To hell with what's happening in the city.''

She grinned. My mother actually grinned. ''Yeah,'' she said, as the first big raindrops fell on our faces. ''To hell with the city.'' She headed down the trail towards home. Then she stopped and looked over her shoulder at me. ''For awhile, anyway.''

# CHAPTER TWENTY-SIX

GRAN had taken the sixteen footer, so we were left with the smaller boat. Its shallow bottom slammed up and down over the choppy waves. It wasn't until we were at the landing in the far bay that it hit me.

"We don't have a car, I'll bet," I said, tying up the boat next to Gran's. I squelched back and forth on the rotting dock. "We're so stupid, we should have brought Gran's keys to her little Rover. Now we don't have a ride."

Mother, her bangs plastered against her forehead, peered through the steady downpour. "I never thought. I have the keys to our car. Maybe they used hers. Tim wouldn't leave us without a car. He's probably going to take the bus."

She was right. The station wagon stood underneath the trees at the end of the trail, littered in leaves, twigs and dead bugs. Good old Tim.

When we parked at the back of the lodge, we found May standing behind the screen door, as if she'd been waiting for us. We slogged through the puddles towards her.

"Thank God, you've come," she breathed. "Tim is upstairs with her now. We're waiting for the doctor."

Mother swung open the door. "What's wrong? Is it Ma?"

"Didn't you see Alex on the road? He was on his way to get Doc and then to get you." May looked grim. "She had one of her funny spells. I think it may be her heart."

"What funny spells? I don't know anything about any funny spells. Did she have a heart attack?"

May was trying hard to be calm, but her hands were wringing a tea towel. "Well, Connie, she's been having these pains the past while. Doc gave her pills that she puts under her tongue. We gave her one and she's lying down. The pain's stopped and she's asleep. She seemed awfully agitated when she came in. She kept insisting that Tim stay and eat with her and when he wouldn't... he said something about the bus...she got even more upset and that's when the pains started."

"Where is he? Is Tim with her? Has he gone already?"

"I'm right here, Connie," said a deep voice beside the stairs. "She's okay. She's asleep."

I ran towards the stairs and he gently caught my arm. "Don't wake her, Lizzie, okay?"

"I have to see her," I said. "I have to see her."

"I know. Just don't wake her up if you can help it."

I nodded dumbly and ran up the stairs. She was

lying on May's chenille bedspread, a down-filled comforter over her long body. Only her knobbly feet stuck out the end. She always likes to keep her feet cool.

I crept up to her side and gazed down at her. Someone had taken her top plate out, and the soft upper lip had sunk in a little. Her colour was bad.

I put one hand over her gnarled fist, but didn't touch it. I wanted to grab it and press it to my face, to feel its warmth, to feel it move. Behind the thin crêpey eyelids, her eyes rolled, then she opened them slowly.

"Lizzie? My teeth, for pete's sake. Get my damn teeth."

I took them out of the glass of water and put them in her hand. Like Harv, she gave them a few clicks before smiling up at me.

"That's better. My, I needed that sleep. I suppose that May's got everybody hysterical? I don't intend to die yet."

"Oh, Gran," was all I could say, "I love you."

Her lids grew heavy again. "If you love me, you'll go make me a cup of tea. I'm dry as a bone. And when the doctor comes tell her to go home."

I shook my head. "No way, Gran."

"We'll start with the tea." Her eyes closed, then opened again. "Then, doctor or no doctor, we're out of here."

"Listen, Gran —"

"And don't forget that tea. I'll get up otherwise. And give me a hug."

152

When I got down to the kitchen, May was hammering away at some bread dough, cursing under her breath.

"Where's Mother and Tim?"

"They've gone outside," she grunted. "Crazy fools. I told them they could use my living room, but no, they had to go out in the rain." She shook her head. "Just as well. I could belt both of them."

I waited for the rest. I knew she wouldn't stop there.

She put her floured hands on her hips. "Your gran cannot take the strain that girl, your mother, puts on her. Has *always* put on her. First she leaves the area without a howdyadoo...hardly ever comes up after she's married. Then when she does come up, she brings this new husband that she's not talking to half the time. Then the husband walks out and gets Terry in a real tizzy and look what happens!"

"Well!" I said hotly, "if you people had told my mother about Gran's being sick maybe we all would have slowed up a little. We love her too, you know. Where's the tea? Gran wants a cup."

We stood in the middle of the room, snorting at each other, then both of us made for the kettle and had a tug of war over it.

"You make your bread, I'll make the tea," I said fiercely.

We glared over the big silver kettle and burst into tears, hugging each other around its big belly.

"Doc's here!" Alex shouted from the yard. A car door slammed and May and I scrambled to let Doc Lindstrom in.

With a curt nod in our direction, she kicked off her muddy boots and walked swiftly to the stairs.

'I'll let you know what's what after I've seen her,'' she said. Her friendly freckled face leaned around the door jamb. "Make us both some tea, will you?''

By the time the kettle was ready, Alex was getting the cups out, cutting up a nut loaf and slapping butter on the slabs.

"Better get your parents,'' he said. "Doc'll want to talk to them.''

I nodded and walked to the front windows overlooking the lake. The rain had changed to a thick misty spray and the wind was gusting heavy curtains of it up and down the bay. I saw Tim's big red rain poncho down by the shore and Mother's blue raincoat moving towards it, becoming engulfed and disappearing inside. Then they walked towards the lodge. I sat down by the fire in the lounge and tried to look casual.

They walked in the door and I could tell from Tim's silly grin that they'd made up. My mother didn't look happy or sad, but her eyes and face seemed to glow from inside. I figured this was a sign that she was willing to give it a try.

"I'll see Gran now that you're down, Lizzie,'' she said, in a determined voice. May handed her a cup of tea to take with her.

The rest of us sat around the kitchen table and waited for the verdict. It didn't take long.

Dorothy Lindstrom, known as Doc to the town of Fish Narrows and two hundred miles surrounding it, rumbled deep in her throat, sat down and said, "I'd like to keep her here for tonight, Connie. Just to check on her every few hours. I could send her to The Pas, but I don't think that will be necessary. Besides, I know she'd fight me all the way."

She looked at each of us in turn, and I felt pinned to my seat when her small brown eyes bored into mine.

"As I told you upstairs, Connie, and I'll tell your husband and daughter, Terry has angina pectoris. She is, after all, over seventy years old, and up to now, she's been doing very well. But I've tried to tell her, if she wants a long life, she *cannot* overdo it."

Tim, Mother and I didn't look at each other, but I could feel their guilt slide onto the table with mine.

"Now," she said, clasping her freckled hands together, "now, with all of you staying for the summer, maybe she's taken on too much. Not that you shouldn't be here. It's just that Terry wants to do it all herself. Now you'll have to do for her. Not treating her like a cripple, mind. But doing the heavy stuff."

The three of us hung our heads and nodded. She slapped the table with her hand and we all jumped guiltily.

"Good! Well, you should be able to have her back under those conditions by tomorrow afternoon. Okay?"

"That's better than we expected," said Mother.

"But remember," said Doc, shaking her finger all

155

around. "There can be no stress in her life right now, eh?"

"Right," we said sheepishly.

"That's settled then. May? I'll send Isa Birch over. She's taking on a few special jobs now she's retired from the nursing home. You and she can keep an eye on Terry." She looked at us. "Anything else comes up, we'll send Alex with a message, okay?"

"Okay," we repeated in turn.

We were back at the landing dock by dusk. As we passed the dark silhouette of Rain Island, barely visible in the darkening mist, I thought of Frances. We'd both cried that day at the thought of losing someone we loved. I hugged my raincoat tighter.

I wondered about two families, many years apart through time, and I thought about how there had been problems on both sides of this strange time curtain that separated us from each other.

It seemed that no matter what time you lived in, you had to face up to things that weren't so great. You couldn't run away from them. I knew that somehow Frances Rain had run away from hers. When I went back to the island, would the girl be gone? Would it all end up with Frances alone again? I wasn't sure I wanted to know. But at least we still had Gran.

The moon slid out from behind a thick bank of clouds, and suddenly I felt very close to Frances, almost as if she rode side by side with me across the misty water.

# CHAPTER TWENTY-SEVEN

ERICA, crazy with happiness to have Tim back, but upset over Gran, slammed back and forth between fits of silliness and angry sobbing all through dinner. She didn't want ham, she wanted ham, no not cut like that, skinny pieces like Gran cut it, sob, sob, sob. I sincerely hoped that Mother and Tim would do something about that whining soon.

Evan, white-faced and silent, made a quiet exit to his room after refusing dessert. I think Gran's illness hit him pretty hard. Mother followed him and returned half an hour later, a bright red spot on each cheek and a gleam in her eye. Round one for those two.

I was so wiped out, I could hardly see straight. At the doorway into the hall, I turned and said, "Do you really think Gran will be okay?"

"She has to be. We won't allow her not to be," she said.

When I saw the look she gave Tim, I was satisfied. I staggered down the hall, and as soon as my comforter fell over me, sleep grabbed me by the ankles and pulled me down into its furry cave. The last sound I heard was the steady patter of rain, like velvet-gloved fingers tapping on the roof.

I peered at the glowing hands of my clock. Three-thirty. What had woken me up? Was it because the rain had stopped, and everything was so quiet? Or had some other noise, some sharp night sound outside my window cut through the silence of my dreams?

The window on the wall across from the foot of my bed was open and the old plaid curtains shifted with the damp breeze that shushed through the silver-edged screen. I burrowed deeper under the comforter. Suddenly I was in one of those awful moments when you are alone and you get that curious feeling that you're *not alone*. I felt goose bumps run up and down my arms like spiders. I could handle ghosts in broad daylight now, but the middle of the night was something else. Too Edgar Allan Poe for words.

I forced myself to think about Gran. And Mother and Tim. And Alex. And about the amazing events of the day. I tried to comfort myself with the thought of Gran returning the next day, but that awful feeling wrapped a little tighter around me.

I held my breath and stared wide-eyed at the wall beside my face. My skin prickled and my scalp tightened. I wondered who was making that horrible, thin, rasping sound until I realized it was me — trying not to breathe. I knew that if I turned over, one of the Rain Island people would be standing beside my bed. I just knew it.

Hero that I am, I screwed my eyes shut and covered my head. The feeling eating at me grew even stronger. Lowering the blanket, I rolled one eye as far as it would go to one side. No one. Slowly, slowly, my neck as stiff as a rusted door handle, I turned to look behind me.

Nothing.

I sat up. There was nobody there at all. With shaking hands, I lit the coal oil lamp beside my bed. Its wavering light shifted and broke across the log walls and over my bed. No one.

I felt a little better until I set down the match box on my bedside table and saw the spectacles. They seemed to shudder and shift in the dim light. Did they move just a little towards me? If I put them on, what would I see? I held them up to my eyes with shaking hands.

Frances and the girl materialized in the darker haze of light at the foot of the bed, their images trembling like the flickering of the flame in my lamp. I pushed my hips back into the pillows and held the covers up to my nose, leaving only my bulging eyes and the glasses above.

Frances was looking straight at me. I felt my breath leave my body in short, sharp bursts. She was holding both her hands in front of her, palms up, and I felt her energy move across the space between us like an electric arc.

One of her hands moved slowly away. Its fingers pointed towards the far wall, in the direction of the island. Over and over again she repeated the gesture. I nodded vigorously, not really knowing why. Her long hair was down around her shoulders in a frizzy mess. She was wearing a long-sleeved nightgown. Her cheeks seemed to have fallen inward and her eyes were deeper, full of shadows. It looked as if it had taken all her strength to lift her arms.

The girl, barely visible, stood beside her, looking around the room with interest, touching the comforter, the bedstead, and her own clothes, a look of wonderment on her shadow face. The coat she was wearing was the same coat she'd arrived in so many years ago. Although she looked in my direction, I didn't think she could see me.

Her image faded first, followed by Frances's, but not before Frances spoke to me once more with her dark, sombre eyes. I nodded with all my might, not knowing if she could see me.

As their delicate hold slowly gave way, I realized with a shock of surprise that they hadn't looked at each other. I wondered if either knew the other was there.

Not removing the spectacles, I lay stiff and still under the covers. I listened and waited, but I knew from the hollowness of the air around me that they were gone. I also knew that I'd go to the island first thing in the morning. If time didn't play a trick on me, tomorrow I'd know what this visit was all about. If Frances came all the way to my cabin, it had to be important. I wondered where she was now.

Outside, a new storm wind moaned through the trees and rain poured down like tears.

# CHAPTER TWENTY-EIGHT

GETTING away wasn't as easy as I thought.

When I opened my glued eyelids, Evan was standing at the edge of my bed, glaring at me. The room was flooded with sunlight.

"You had to go and do a Dear Abby on those two, didn't you?" he snarked. "Now, I'll have to put up with tuna casseroles for good. God, I *hate* tuna casseroles."

I stared at him through one eye. "Shut up, Evan. You're as glad as we are to have him back. And get out of my room." I was in no mood for this particular earthly visitation.

He stood his ground. "You saw Gran? How did she look?" He was biting his bottom lip, and I took pity.

"She looked okay," I said. "Doc Lindstrom says she'll be fine. She demanded a cup of tea the minute I saw her." I sat up and stretched. "She'll be okay. Honest."

"Are you bulling me?" he demanded, his voice cracking.

"No. She looked tired, but she'll be fine. Really. Truly."

"Yeah, well, you better not be bulling me," he growled and walked out slamming the door behind him.

I smiled at the ceiling. Soon, he'd be almost human.

I got dressed quickly, hoping to avoid a crush in the kitchen. They'd beat me to it. Just my luck. Tim was toasting bread over the open grate in the cookstove and Mother was buttering the pieces. They touched at every opportunity. Now and again she'd glance over at her gaping kids, smile apologetically and then smile again. It was as if she was keeping some private secret to herself. So did Tim.

When they weren't looking, Evan made silent gagging gestures, pointing deep into his throat, then clutching his neck, tongue hanging out. After a few minutes of watching the two old coots, I felt in complete sympathy with him.

"You wanna go fishing?" he asked testily.

"No thanks. I don't feel so hot. I think I'll just bum around."

"Suit yourself. Boat needs bailing anyway." He shrugged.

"If I bail the boat, can I go?" asked Erica. "Please?"

He rolled his eyes. "I guess so. If you bail the boat."

"Oh, goody! I'll go now."

"You can help her bail, Evan," said Mother, sweetly smiling.

Evan rolled his eyes again, glared at Tim and slouched out behind Erica, who was skipping through the kitchen door.

"No point in hoping to change him overnight," Tim sighed.

"Still, isn't this nice? He's practising for when Ma gets home. He'll soon realize he doesn't have to be a tough guy all the time," Mother said, fondly. "I'll have to get a little tougher to match him. And spend more time with him. And the girls. Like you've been doing."

"Jeez, don't get too chummy," I said. "We're not used to it. Just be there when we *do* need you. Cripes. Listen to me. I sound like something from my grade ten guidance book."

Tim grinned and flipped my pony tail. "Don't worry. We'll never turn into the Cosby family. Somehow I'm still outnumbered by McGills."

Mother cleared her throat. "So, what are you going to do today, Lizzie?"

It was my turn to grin. "Oh, I thought I'd hang around you guys." I saw the look that passed between them. "Okay, okay, I can take a hint. I'm going out in the canoe. For, oh...let's say a couple of hours? Have fun!"

"Kids these days know too damn much," growled Tim, tossing me a piece of buttered toast. I took it on the run and headed out the door.

On the island, leaves glistened from last night's rain and the white reindeer moss, usually crusty and dry, was soft and spongy under my sneakers.

When I put the glasses on, I found the girl standing not far from me on the landing rock. She was waving to Frances, who had just pushed off from shore in a loaded-down canoe. Frances was dressed in a plaid jacket and knitted hat. She waved back, then dug her paddle deep into the water, pulling towards Gran's shore. A few strokes later, she turned and called something to the girl, who shook her head, laughed and waved her away. I had the feeling that she wanted to take the girl with her, but I couldn't see how, when the canoe was so full of supplies.

That's when it came to me that they might be changing camps. If Frances was going on ahead to set up another place, perhaps in one of her trapping cabins, then they must be worried about the Toad Man coming back. Still, I was only guessing. But it made a lot of sense.

When Frances turned back to her paddling, I was disappointed that she didn't look my way. Had she forgotten last night? Did she know I was here? What about her message?

A gust of wind pulled a million yellow leaves off the trees along the shore. Many of the trees stood naked already, their bare skeletons stark against the sky.

The girl watched the canoe get smaller and smaller. When it was just a dot, she got up and walked slowly towards the cabin. I sat where I was, watching her, wondering idly what her name was. She didn't look like a Jane or a Nellie, or even a Hildegard. I watched while she collected wood.

After that, when she sat down to read, I sat across from her and sketched her in soft blue pencil. She seemed to suit blue because she was so much harder to see than Frances. I wondered why.

I was just putting in the lines of her shirt sleeves, when she put down the book and stared out over the lake in the opposite direction to the way Frances had gone. I craned my neck to see what she was looking at. A speck on the horizon was moving steadily in our direction.

She dropped her book and ran into the cabin, coming out almost immediately with Frances's binoculars. She stiffened. When she lowered the glasses, her eyes had the frozen stare of a deer caught in the headlights of an oncoming car. Leaning into the wind that had suddenly picked up, she looked in the direction that Frances's freighter canoe had gone. For some reason, her figure became clearer then, as if in her fear she had taken on new energy.

As the vessel moved closer, I recognized the twins at either end. They wore the same blue shirts under matching mackinaws. Their canoe cut through the deep waves like a well-honed cleaver. In the middle, between the twins, wearing the same coat and fedora, sat the Toad Man.

# CHAPTER TWENTY-NINE

THE Toad Man levered himself onto the dock, stood up to his full height and adjusted his coat on his shoulders. He started up the path to the cabin. I looked around. The girl was gone.

Wide grey shoulders suddenly blocked my vision, and like an animated character on a movie screen, he shimmered past me and up the path. I ran beside him calling out, "Frances will be back soon. Wait for her. Don't take the girl yet. Frances doesn't know!"

But he didn't hear me. He plodded on, relentless as a chain saw cutting through a slab of pine.

In my rush to help her, I forgot that although the path would be clear going for them, it wasn't for me. My foot slid under a hidden root and I was flat on my face, my sketchbook landing in the undergrowth beside me. From that position I watched him walk into the cabin.

By the time I reached the door it was shut. The handle dissolved under my hand. I ran to the side window and peered in. The girl stood staring at the man as he flung things into her old suitcase. Finally, she ran to him, pulling on his arm, but he brushed her off like a pesky mosquito.

When he was done, he looked around to make sure he had everything, then pulled her coat off the peg and handed it to her. She shook her head, her arms stiff by her sides, her chin in the air. He shook it at her and said something, his frog lips barely moving. I saw a row of small pointed teeth. She shook her head and said something back, something that must have shocked both of them, because they stood face to face like statues. Then, he raised his huge hand and slapped her.

When he turned away from her, I saw anguish on his face at what he'd done. Yet he hunched his shoulders, set his angry expression and faced her again, towering over her like a monstrous reptile. Slowly, without a word, tears running down her face, she put on the coat.

He lunged out of the cabin, leaving the door swinging on its hinges. A splash of sunlight fell on the girl. She was tying on her hat with shaking fingers. I was sure I heard her faint sobbing in my head. I smelled wood smoke and looked up to see it pouring out of the tin chimney. The wind dragged it over the roof and tumbled it into the nearby trees.

The girl was walking around the room, touching first a little vase of autumn leaves, next a wooden rocker and a small bed in the corner. I strained towards the glass. The bed was exactly the same as the one in my room at Gran's. It was my bed!

Before I could wrap that discovery around my brain cells, the girl knelt down and pulled something out from under the mattress. It was a small, flat shape, wrapped in what looked like soft chamois. She was heading towards the small blue table by the front window when the Toad Man burst into the cabin again. He grabbed her by the wrist and pulled her outside.

As I stumbled after them down the path, I could hear the ghostly murmur of the long-ago wind that tore at their coats, propelling them towards the canoe and waiting men. The poor girl was trying to tell him something; she kept pulling back and waving the parcel with her free hand. He kept shaking his head, dragging her along with him. The two Indians watched with closed faces.

The girl leaned her weight back and away from the Toad Man, but her feet skittered down the rocky slope. When she fell forward with one final pull of his strong arm, the parcel dropped to the ground. She tried to grab at it, but in the scuffle, the Toad Man's foot kicked it, and it disappeared over the sharp edge of the rocks.

Overcome, the girl was led to the canoe and lifted in. The big man followed close behind, the canoe dipping under his weight. The girl fell back against the thwart, her face covered by her hands.

As they pulled away, I ran to the shore and cried, ''I'll tell her! I promise. I'll tell her what happened. I promise!'' But she didn't look up.

The canoe with its gentle prisoner rode into the haze of the autumn sky. While I cried, the summer visions of my own world grew stronger, blotting out the pale shimmering yellows of her past.

I don't know how long I sat with my arms and head resting on my knees. The past few weeks crowded in on me. How much more could a person stand?

My mind was in such turmoil, it was like a roar of wind in my ears. Then, under the roar, came the faint far drone of the motor. Confused, I looked in the direction the big canoe had taken.

In the distance, skimming past the island was a small boat, and in it were two people, one a tall thin figure wearing a wide straw hat. The other was Alex. He was driving Gran home. It took me less than a minute to climb into the Beetle and push out into the sun-dappled water. I waved, using both arms. When they waved back, I felt my heart swell. I figured I could stand a bit more after all.

# CHAPTER THIRTY

ALEX stayed for lunch and somehow ended up playing poker with Tim and Evan afterwards. Mother sat reading Tim's mystery, peering over the top of it like a private detective in a hotel lobby. Need I say that Tim and Evan had loudly different rules to the game? I could hear the squabbling from the veranda where I was sitting with Gran.

"Humph!" she said, tossing aside the diet sheet Doc had given her. "I baked that chocolate cake yesterday because it's *my* favourite. This diet business is for the birds."

"It didn't look too bad," I said, encouragingly.

"Humph."

"How do you feel?"

"Fine. Just fine. Don't fuss, Lizzie."

I sat down on the end of her lounge. "Just fine? Oh, yeah? Let's try that again. How do you feel?"

"Lousy. Tired," she muttered. "Old, worn-out and cheesed-off."

"That's about normal, isn't it?" She gave me a beady-eyed look. "Did you sleep okay at May's?"

"You know, Lizzie, it's the funniest thing...silly really...but when I was a young woman, I used to have these funny dreams. And last night I had them again. Could be the pills I'm taking."

"You mean, funny ha, ha, or funny weird?"

She leaned against the cushion, closing her eyes. "Funny weird."

"Me too. I had weird dreams, too. What were yours about, Gran?"

Her voice was husky with tiredness. "Just very strange. It's always the same. It's like I'm standing off a bit watching. A girl is standing at the foot of my bed and she's looking at everything in the room. And in my bed is another girl. Not me. Or is she? I want to talk to them, but I know I can't. They don't see me. I have something important to tell them. Then I wake up and I can't remember what it is. Funny." Her voice faded into a whisper, and she was asleep.

I held her long bony hand in mine and did some hard but frazzled thinking. Wasn't this the same dream I had had the night before? Except she didn't mention Frances being there. Why would Gran have a dream so much like mine? I laid her hand gently over the other one and tiptoed into the cabin. Alex was in the kitchen getting Cokes.

"Alex. I've got to talk to you."

He put his arms on my shoulders, a Coke can in each hand. "About time. Thought I'd developed halitosis of the worst kind. Don't frown. I'm just kidding." He aimed a kiss at the proper spot, but I turned my head and it missed.

"Alex. I've got to talk to you!"

He looked around. "Is there a parrot in here? Or an echo?"

"Alex! I've...."

"I know, I know — talk to me." He walked to the door. "Hey guys, deal me out. Elizabeth and I are going for a walk."

"Jeez, Birdface, real poker players don't leave in the middle of the game, especially when they're winning," called Evan.

"Yeah, Bird. Get in here and deal. My luck's changing," growled Tim.

"Sorry, fellas. I'm out."

"Deal me in, then," said Mother from behind her book.

"Women can't play poker," sneered Evan. "Especially Mothers."

"We'll see who has the most matchsticks at the end," she said.

"Me, too, I'll play too," chimed in Erica from the floor where she'd been colouring. That was followed by an elaborate groan.

Alex and I walked out the back door.

"One big happy family, eh?" said Alex. "Think it'll last?"

"Who knows?" At that moment I didn't care if they attacked each other with axes. "Listen, I have to tell you something."

"No kidding," he said, laughing.

I pushed him and he grabbed me and we walked along the shore hand in hand. I told him as clearly as I could what had happened the night before, and on the island that afternoon, and finally about Gran's dream.

"That's kind of spooky, Lizzie, eh? You both had the same one?"

"Sort of. But mine wasn't a dream," I insisted. "I woke up, put on the glasses and that's when I saw them. But I'm sure that Frances and the girl didn't see each other. And I'm sure I didn't dream it. So you can stop looking like that."

"Could you somehow have connected into your gran's dream? Or she into yours?"

"I didn't dream it!"

"Okay, okay. Did you look for this parcel that the girl dropped?"

"The parcel!" I cried. "I never even thought to look! I was too upset. We've got to find it!"

"Hey, Liz, wait."

But I was running to the dock. "I've got the specs in my pocket. That's all I need."

When we landed on the island, Alex said, "What if Frances already found it? I mean, sixty years ago. Cripes, I'm talking like they're here now!" He pulled the nose of the boat onto shore. "Or it could have fallen into the water and rotted away."

"On the other hand," I called over my shoulder as I ran up the slope, "it could still be here."

There was a fairly steep drop on one side of the landing rock. The rock itself had split and cracked into layers, and the sheared-off blocks and slates were lying in a jumbled mass down the slope and in the water below.

Little secret ledges lay one on top of the other,

some deep and dark, others shallow and glowing with brightly coloured moss and berries. My heart sank. "I saw it slide over here. It probably landed in the lake."

"Which side was she standing on?"

"She wasn't standing. The big bully was dragging her, and she dropped it right where you're standing. It went on an angle when he kicked it. That way." I pointed to his left sneaker.

"It could have fired into one of those ledges, then," he said, getting down on his knees and leaning over the edge.

I ask you. What more could a person ask for? You tell a guy that one of the ghosts you've been watching for a couple of weeks — through a pair of antique specs, no less — dropped a parcel, and he helps you look for it.

I hopped and crossed the jagged stones, feeling their sharp edges through the soles of my sneakers. All around the rock face were dark holes, broken ledges and tufts of moss with little green ferns growing out of them.

"Here's a pretty deep crevice," I called back. "Seems to go straight in. Darn! I wish I had a flashlight."

"Flashlight?" asked Alex, who was lying on his stomach, chin on arms, peering down at me. "Got one in the boat. I'll get it."

I peered anxiously into the dark, flat hole, and waited. A few minutes later, a flashlight dangled before my eyes on a thin stretch of fishing line.

"You could have handed it down," I said, laughing.

"I know. But the Hardy Boys or Nancy Drew would have been hanging over a two hundred foot drop looking for treasure and someone would lower a light to them. On a rope. Just wanted to get into the spirit of the thing."

I untied the flashlight. "Very funny." Just beyond my reach, the dim glow of the flash picked up a blackened block of something. "Hey! Wait! Get down here."

Alex's reach was just long enough. He brought it out, dragging dirt and leaves with it.

"She sure liked to wrap things in leather," I said softly.

"My God, Lizzie," he said, "you really *did* see her drop this all those years ago. Let's get up there and open it."

I was out of breath after clambering to the top and sat down with a thump. The day was warm and sunny, but the little parcel felt cold and heavy in my hand.

"Maybe whatever it is will crumble away when I touch it," I muttered, turning it over in my hands.

"Will you open the stupid thing? The suspense is killing me." He fell back, making death rattles.

I slowly unwound the blackened leather thong that held it together. The buckskin was dark and stiff, and held its shape. Under it was a layer of oil cloth. I pulled it away. I don't know what I was expecting, but this wasn't it. Was this the same flat sketchbook I'd seen her drawing in? My heart was beating hard and fast.

"It's just an old sketchbook," said Alex. "See? There's a long fabric loop with a pencil still in it. Hey, nice pencil. Gold, I bet. It isn't even rusted. Do you think the lead still works?"

I wasn't listening. I opened the flap. Inside was a slender pile of yellowed pages, water spotted and covered in fine writing and delicate drawings — some in pencil, some in ink, and here and there the faint blush of water colours.

It was a picture and word diary of the girl's stay on Rain Island. The cabin, sketched in ink, the lake painted in soft spring colours, a pencil sketch of dark thunderclouds, were all surrounded by writing, a kind of recording of each day's events. The last entry had been made the day before the Toad Man returned.

Frances is going over tomorrow to set up a place for us in a small cabin she has on Form Lake. We'll leave in a day or two, just in case Papa decides to fool us and come early. When the snow lies deep on the lake, we'll return to our little home on the island. I can hardly wait to see Rain Lake under the safe cloak of winter. I have two more pages to fill and then I will give this little book to Frances. She worries that I'm lonely here. She'll see how much I truly belong here. With her.

I turned the pages as if they were made out of butterfly wings. If only she had gone with Frances, chances are she would have stayed clear of Papa, the Toad Man. When I was about to close the cover, I saw an inscription. It said, "To Frances Rain, my mother. A New Beginning. Lovingly, from your daughter, Teresa, 1925."

"Her name was Teresa," I said wonderingly. "Finally I know her name. She wasn't Frances's sister or niece, but her daughter!"

"So the man Teresa calls Papa is really Frances's father?" suggested Alex. "Papa must stand for Grandpa."

I looked at him. I'd forgotten he was there.

"But didn't Frances Rain die in 1925? Isn't that what Harv said?" he asked.

"That's right! And the sketchbook is dated 1925."

Alex thought for a moment. "She must have died soon after Teresa left."

I nodded. It was so much to take in at once. My senses seemed to go into shock, then reorganize themselves until I could think, and then my skin felt hot and cold at the same time, and then I couldn't think at all. Something was screaming at me to take notice. It was Alex who brought everything to a grinding halt.

"What was her name?" He gripped my arm. "What was the girl's name?"

"Teresa," I said, as if in a dream. "Teresa Rain. Maybe it wasn't Rain. I wonder if they called her Terry..." That was the moment when everything slid into place. Gran.

# CHAPTER THIRTY-ONE

"I THINK that your spirit girl and Terry, your gran, are one and the same, Lizzie," Alex said. "What did Frances find when she returned? Nothing! Not even a note."

"The Toad Man kept looking at his watch," I remembered. "While he was pushing her along. He must have had someone waiting to whisk them away. The trains used to come as far as Poplar Hills Station, and I'll bet those guides had a fast way out. I wonder if Frances planned on following her back east? Maybe she thought Teresa had deserted her? No note. . .no nothing. How did she stand it?" I held his arm. "How did she die?"

"She didn't, remember?" Alex said quietly. "She's still here. Put the spectacles on. I'll go wait in the boat."

"I. . .can't. . .I. . . ."

"Put them on, Lizzie. Or you'll always be wondering."

He was right. I was afraid, but I had to finish this.

Alex touched my cheek with his fingertips, then turned and walked away.

Clutching the book against my chest with one hand, I used the other to put on the glasses. As I walked up the slope and into the pines, I felt the change. It was completely different.

Frances's cabin came slowly into focus. I felt my hair fly back with a blast of freezing air. Autumn was over. It was night. The snow lay thick on the roof and had piled in smooth banks around the low walls.

I felt the sting of bitter cold as it cut into my face and through my thin shirt. Ahead of me, snow as fine as flour swirled off the trees, blocking out the cabin for a few seconds. With the moment of clearing, the wide blue snowdrifts seemed to shift and breathe around the darkened logs, and a pale light from a window picked out the falling crystals.

Someone was home, yet there were no footprints in the layer of smooth snow ahead. I walked towards the cabin, feeling my feet bump over blueberry bushes, rocks and fallen logs below the ghostly snow. At last, I stood waist deep in snow at the front door.

This time when I touched the handle, I felt its roughness under my fingers. I pushed against the door. It was like pushing against a damp sponge. I almost fell forward when it opened inwards. Snow fell in clumps onto the floor at my feet. I quickly shut it behind me, using all my strength. Finally, I heard a faint far-off click as its lock shut.

A fire burned low in the grate, and I was glad to feel its faint warmth. Beside the fire, a small bed had been pulled close. Someone was lying in the bed I'd slept in so many summers.

In the flickering firelight, I saw the bookshelves crammed with books, the little blue table by the window, and fur rugs on the wood floor. Behind me, hanging on the wall, were the stretchers and traps I'd seen Frances working on.

I looked at the woman on the bed. Her face was as familiar as my own. Her eyes were closed, and the black hair along her forehead was curly and damp with sweat. In her sleep, she frowned and her hands moved restlessly back and forth on top of the covers. The gold signet ring gleamed in the firelight. She moved a hand to her mouth and coughed. It echoed in the silent room.

Slowly her eyes opened and she turned her head to look at me. I laid the sketchbook in her hands. When her fingers closed over it, I felt a tingly shock run up my arms. Her face was deep with shadows and her thin body hardly made a rise under the covers. She tried to lift the book, but its weight sagged beneath her almost lifeless fingers. She looked at me in despair.

Kneeling beside her, I opened the book and held it up for her to see the inscription. She lifted her head to speak, and fell back exhausted, but there was a fire in her eyes. They followed the writing on each page and the bloodless lids opened in amazement when she realized what she was looking at.

Page by page, I watched her drink in what her daughter had done. The last drawing in the book was of Frances, sitting and reading at the little blue table, her moccasined feet resting on the lower rungs of the chair.

Frances's finger lifted from the bedcovers and touched the drawing, and she read the short paragraph beside it. Her eyes travelled up to my face and she studied it closely.

"I'm Lizzie," I said.

She nodded. She knew. She fought to keep her eyes open, but the heavy lids closed. I didn't know what to do. I felt so helpless. It was then that I felt her fingers wrap around my wrist. It was the same feeling as when a spider web clings to you, light, yet curiously strong.

She opened her mouth to speak. I leaned close to her face and felt her breath stir my hair.

"I left everything too late." She touched the sketchbook. "Give this to Teresa, my dearest girl. Tell her I've seen it. Tell her I would have come."

I heard the words as though down a long tunnel, faint yet clear as crystal, "I would have come."

I nodded, not daring to speak, took the book and backed slowly away. Her face, relaxed now, was beautiful and calm in the firelight. I walked forward again and touched her open hand with my fingertips. Her fingers closed over mine, then released them and her eyes fluttered open.

They followed me as I walked to the door. How could I leave her? I started back towards the bed and the warmth of the fire, but she held up her hand to stop me. Outside the snow touched the windows and melted, their tears slowly moving down the glass. I clutched the book closer to me, and as the images around me began to fade, I wanted to cry out, ''Not yet, not yet.''

I hadn't even got to know her, really. I'd only seen her through a few dreamlike days. Nobody had got to know my great-grandmother very well, except maybe the girl. Terry. My gran.

Our eyes met across the room and we said goodbye in our hearts, and then she was gone. I found myself standing in the middle of the cabin site, the tears still wet on my face, the sketchbook in my hands.

# CHAPTER THIRTY-TWO

ALEX said nothing when I stumbled to the shore, but I felt his arm go around my shoulders. After my sobbing slowed down to a few choking gulps, he helped me into the boat and handed me a grubby cloth from under the seat to mop up my face.

Tying up at Gran's a few minutes later, he said, "I saw the Happy Gang, all four of them, over on Whisky Rock picking berries. So they're out of the way. I'll stay here, on the dock while you talk to Terry, okay?"

I bit my lip and nodded. I had to carry out Frances's last wish. Halfway up the path, I stopped. How could I tell my practical, down-to-earth grandmother that I'd just shown her sketchbook to her dying mother? I'd have to think something up. Like maybe the tooth fairy gave it to me.

I found her in her bedroom, lying under the same comforter I'd just seen on my great-grandmother's bed. My bed.

"Elizabeth. Good. Someone to talk to. Listen, explain to your family that I won't drop dead if they talk to me. I'm getting awfully bored. Now what. . . ." She stared at the sketchbook and sat up. "Where did you get that?"

All I could say was, "You're Frances Rain's daughter. You visited her when you were a girl and you left this behind."

"How. . .when. . .?"

"Don't get too upset, Gran."

"I'm *not* upset, where. . .?" Her hands reached out.

"The doctor said no stress. I shouldn't have surprised you with this. I should have talked to you first. Are you okay?"

"For heaven's sake, Lizzie, will you shut up? I'm not going to fall over dead. But I will, out of spite, if you don't tell me where you found that!" She struggled to sit up farther. "The Pepins gave me everything that they'd taken from the cabin after she died."

"Alex and I have been excavating her cabin. We found this in a tin box. They must have missed it. It's in good shape, huh?"

"You found it *in* her cabin? You mean she saw it?" Her face split into a wide, incredulous grin. "She *did* find it. She *did* know how much I loved it there. Frances didn't talk much, you see. It was hard for her."

She was quiet for a moment and I knew she was once again standing on the landing rock that first day, her grandfather and the canoe disappearing in the distance, her mother walking away from her up the path.

"But then," she continued, blinking and shaking her head, "you don't know what on earth I'm blathering on about, do you?"

"Why didn't you ever tell anyone you were her daughter? Why didn't you tell me?"

She picked at a thread on the quilt. "Frances wanted it that way. Her pride wouldn't let her tell anyone around here that she had borne an illegitimate child. The man was a prominent politician in Winnipeg. And he was married."

"So no one knows?"

She shook her head. "The Pepins knew. I got in touch with them when I came up north. They'd kept everything for me for years. Of course, they're both dead now." She looked at the sketchbook. "And for years, I thought she'd decided not to come and get me. That she didn't want me."

"The Papa in the book is my great great?"

"Yes. He was a very bitter man and he made sure I knew that my mother was a fallen woman . . .who'd hated the sight of her sickly baby."

"You were sick?"

"I had a heart murmur. In those days that was tantamount to living on the edge of death. At least that's what Papa wanted Frances to believe. He used it against her — a punishment for humiliating him in his closed little middle-class world. He'd warned her that if she took me, it would surely kill me."

"When did you first meet her?"

"One day, when I was nine, she came to our new place in Calgary. Papa had opened a grocery store

185

there. Grandma was dying and she wanted to see Frances one last time.''

"Did you talk to her much?''

"She wasn't a talker, my mother. But I knew when she looked at me that she didn't hate me as Papa said she did.''

"What happened?''

"She took me to the doctor, who reassured her that when I was about thirteen, I would probably be over this heart problem. So Frances went to Papa and said that she wanted me with her. He said my death would be on her hands. That he knew me better than some doctor. She believed him. She left the day of Grandma's funeral.''

"But he finally brought you to see her?''

"How do you know that?''

I poked a finger at the book. "This.''

"Oh, right.''

"So how come he agreed?''

She smiled. "Frances wrote to him when I was thirteen. She said that there would be no more money if he didn't bring me up here. His grocery and hardware store wasn't doing very well. She'd sent him a lot of money over the years. I suspect that he painted a picture of poverty and starvation for her poor little girl. He was like that. I had no idea she'd been sending money all those years. For me.''

"And he used your heart problem to keep you with him?''

"Or he kept me with him to finance his failing business.'' She smiled bitterly. "He was supposed to bank the money for me. But he spent it all on the business."

"Did he leave you anything when he died?"

"There wasn't anything to leave except the store, and he willed that to some cousins in Winnipeg."

"Well," I said. "At least you had Rain Island."

She nodded. "He hoped that the trip would make me too weak to stay. I fooled him. I just got better and better. I kept asking Frances why I couldn't stay for good, but she'd just shake her head. Then one day, she returned from a supply trip and said she'd sent him a letter telling him that I'd be staying the winter. Until spring. I was ecstatic, but I could see she was worried about his temper. She got very broody about it."

"She figured he'd come and get you?"

"Yes. He needed me. To punish her for everything that had gone wrong in his life. He blamed her for everything."

"And here I thought I'd like to live in the past," I said, "to get away from my family. At least my family is still talking. Sort of."

"Oh, you'll be okay, the bunch of you. Frances and my grandfather never patched things up. That's no way to live. Or die."

"He must have really hated her, eh?" I said in awe.

"Hated her? Or loved her too much. I don't know. He'd tried for years to smother her independence, to keep her near him. He left Winnipeg because he couldn't stand the shame, he said. But it was to take me as far away from her as possible."

"And that's why he had to come back to Rain Island. He couldn't stand to see you two happy together."

"That's right. How *do* you know all this?"

"A wild guess?" I said, hopefully.

She eyed me suspiciously. "Humph. Now, give me the book."

I handed it to her and watched while the pages slowly turned.

"When she didn't write me after I was forced to leave, I thought she must have stopped caring. For months I waited for her to write. Papa kept telling me I was better off without her."

"She'd never have stopped caring," I said softly.

"I guess I knew in my heart she wouldn't forget me. When I found out she'd been dead for months and he hadn't told me, we had a terrible fight. At the time, I really believed he had arranged her death."

"Really?"

She gave me a thin smile. "We never spoke of it again, but when I was nineteen, I left him and came here to teach. Just as she had. Four years later, I married your Grandpa Bill. A man as different from my grandfather as one can get — didn't care two pins for getting rich. I tracked down the doctor who'd done the autopsy. Mother died of pneumonia. If I'd been here I might have helped her. That was another reason for not forgiving Papa."

"And what happened to him?"

"He died a year after I moved here. He'd never

have understood Frances or me if he'd lived to be a hundred." She sighed. "I guess I'm no better with my own daughter. Connie's always been so different from me. Frances and I were painted with the same brush. I had hoped.. . ."

She sagged back into her pillows.

"But you can't make someone into something you want them to be," I said. "That's what you've always told me."

Her eyes were still on me, but she wasn't seeing me. She was working out something in her mind. "Yes," she said, finally. "Yes, I have told you that. Too bad I couldn't take my own advice. But maybe it's not too late. Maybe Connie and I can get to know each other again." She hesitated, then pointed across the room. "Open up that top drawer, the little one in the middle. Bring me the small wooden box. That's it. Open it."

I couldn't help it — I gasped. It lay on a piece of soft suede, smooth and golden, its band worn thin at the back. In the middle of the flat gold face, I could make out a faint but clear scrolled F. It was Frances Rain's signet ring.

# CHAPTER THIRTY-THREE

"IT'S yours now," she said, matter-of-factly. "You and I can share her memory. She'd like that." I tried to argue but she held up her long hand. "It was sent to my grandfather. I found it in his desk a few months after I'd returned to live with him. That's when I knew she was dead."

I slipped it onto my middle finger. I felt warm and tingled a bit.

"I have something else for you, Gran," I said. I took the spectacles out of my pocket and handed them to her.

"Well, for heaven's sake," she said. She put them on the end of her nose and pushed them back. For one brief moment, I saw the long narrow face of the girl from Rain Island. Then she took them off and she was Gran again. Pale and tired. She lay back on her pillows. "Poor Frances. All alone at the end."

"Gran? What are you going to do this winter? I could stay with you. Go to school here." I sat down facing her and put my head on her bony chest. "I don't want you to be alone like Frances."

She laid a large hand over my head. "I've got that all worked out, honey. May and I talked it over when I was there yesterday. I'll move in with her. We're both getting on and she could do with some help on her quilting during those long winter days. I'll sell the house in Fish Narrows. And you'll be with me next summer. Won't you?''

I nodded, my head moving under her hand. I was too busy snuffling to say anything.

''I'll wait till you come back, don't you worry. May says you can work at the lodge over the next month or so to get your feet wet. Then if you want to, you can work steady there next summer.''

I looked up. ''But. . . .''

''It'll be just like always, only better. And don't forget, Alex will need a place to stay in Winnipeg when he goes to university after next summer's over. Who knows? Anything can happen, eh? You have an extra room in that house of yours. Would save him a lot of money.''

I wiped my eyes and grinned. The sound of voices, loud arguing voices, floated through the window beside us. *They* were back.

''Now go and get your family and bring them here. Tell Tim I wish to be escorted to the living room for tea and that chocolate cake. Okay, okay. Tea and toast for me. Even so, I'm awfully hungry.'' She pushed pins into the small knot of hair on the top of her head and smoothed the sides with her hands. ''I'm thirsty as a drunk on payday.''

We laughed like two kids with a wonderful secret. Maybe someday I'd tell her about the Rain Island ghosts. For now, it was just plain wonderful to know that the girl I'd been watching and worrying about — my girl from Rain Island — had been with me all my life. And to know that Frances was finally at peace.

I ran out of the house and down the path, my feet barely touching the ground. The boat, filled with its grumbling passengers, was just nudging up to the dock. A pot of blueberries had spilled all over the bottom of the boat. Erica was wailing, so it wasn't hard to tell whose it was.

"If you'd waited two more seconds before lurching all around the place, Evan, this wouldn't have happened," growled Tim, shutting off the motor. The boat glanced off the dock and hit the shore with a bump.

Three other pails slid around on the seat and Mother lunged at them.

"If you'd quit swinging the boat back and forth," snarled Evan, "I wouldn't have slipped and hit the stupid pail." He moaned loudly at the purple juice squashed against the white canvas of his sneakers. "Damn!"

"Now, Evan, what have I told you about your language?" said mother, underlining a few words with her voice.

"Baaah!" howled Erica, pointing at the crushed berries under her feet.

I stood on the end of the dock, grinning. Alex tiptoed towards me and said, "Is everything all right?"

I laughed. "Well, I've got some good news about Gran and May. And you and me. At least I think you'll think it's good. So. . .is everything all right?" I looked over my shoulder at my family. "I wouldn't have it any other way."